William Sharp, Thomas A. (Thomas Allibone) Janvier

Flower o' the Vine; Romantic Ballads and Sospiri di Roma...

William Sharp, Thomas A. (Thomas Allibone) Janvier

Flower o' the Vine; Romantic Ballads and Sospiri di Roma...

ISBN/EAN: 9783744787529

Printed in Europe, USA, Canada, Australia, Japan

Cover: Foto ©Andreas Hilbeck / pixelio.de

More available books at **www.hansebooks.com**

William Sharp

" *Earth is my* [illegible] *ew there.*"

BROWNING.

FLOWER O' THE VINE:
ROMANTIC BALLADS AND SOSPIRI DI ROMA: BY WILLIAM SHARP: WITH INTRODUCTION BY THOMAS A. JANVIER

CHARLES L. WEBSTER AND COMPANY
PUBLISHERS NEW YORK MDCCCXCII

R

PRESS OF
JENKINS & McCOWAN,
NEW YORK.

INTRODUCTION

In accordance with a courtly usage that is founded in common sense (as is the rule with courtly usages, though Democrats rail to the contrary) letters of introduction are held to be a necessary portion of the equipment of a gentleman who is about to set forth upon his travels in foreign lands. For the most part, to be sure, the traveller may go happily enough without such credentials ; and on his own merits make for himself —supposing him to be truly gentle, and of a cordial quality—all the friends whom he desires by the way. But now and again—as in the case of some ill-bred fellow questioning suddenly his antecedents—his letters will be useful to prove shortly to strangers that in his own country he is a person of condition ; and still more often will he find pleasure in exhibiting them, in proof of his worthiness, to those who frankly have given him their confident friendship without asking for other evidence of his merit than himself.

I take it that from this custom in regard to wandering humans, flows the like custom of supplying with letters commendatory those wandering books which—by translation into a foreign tongue, or by transplanting in their vernacular idiom into a foreign country—chal-

lenge the attention of new friends (or enemies) beyond the limits of their own natural frontiers. Yet, very evidently, a book stands much less in need of such certification than does a man; for the purpose of a man not seldom is to conceal his meaning, and always is to conceal his defects, from those around him; while a book—preëminently of all things created—testifies to and most openly displays its own inherent quality whether the same be good or bad. In the case of the book, therefore, the ceremony of presentation by a common acquaintance has at its root a phase of a still more kindly meaning: for it is less an offer of safe conduct through a region where may lurk annoyances, and even dangers, than it is a prompt display of welcoming friendliness—what may be termed, in metaphor, a flying down to the coast on the part of some one citizen of that new strange country in eager haste to manifest the warmth of his good will (and also, perhaps, to catch a little reflected glory) by being the very first to greet the oncoming distinguished personage as he steps ashore.

Holding these views in the premises, I esteem as a high and agreeable privilege my present opportunity thus to welcome, while in appearance introducing to my fellow countrymen, the Poet whose verses begin a page or two farther on. I say "in appearance" to introduce, for I am not so dull as to fancy that any word of *this matter of mine will be heeded until the essential substance of the Poems to which, nominally, it is precedent shall have been read and re-read with delight; nor am I at all disposed to pick a quarrel with those who may smile a little at the spectacle of a herald thus sounding his trumpet at the wrong end of the line. On the contrary, I am well pleased to occupy that position for the reason that it is a very secure one. Coming as a sequel, rather than as a foreword, this note of mine is to be rated with the letter of introduction (just now spoken of) which is tendered after an acquaintance has been opened and a friendship fairly begun without its aid : that is to say, so far as the practical requirements of the situation go—the friendship being established beyond a peradventure—it is unnecessary ; yet has it a chance of being read with interest, and more than willingly, in the hope that it may throw yet more light upon the personality of the newly found friend. And, moreover, because of the certainty that what I here write will be approached (out of its too-arrogant order) by those who already have apprehended the excellencies of the Poems, I am confident that my readers will sympathize with me in the pleasure that I have in formally presenting to their consideration work of so fine and of so unusual a sort.*

William Sharp has a great deal of personality. As Skybele wrote of Sir Potter Towson, he is " a man of magnificent measurements" ; his vigorous spirit is in keeping with its large bodily frame, and both his soul and body still are elate with the triumphant impulses of youth. His nationality is proclaimed positively in the first poem in this volume : only a Scotsman could have written " The Weird of Michael Scott." But while born of substantial Paisley stock, and bred for half his lifetime in Scotland, his years of journeying and residence in foreign countries have made him very much a citizen of the world. His earlier travels were by no means conventional : a voyage to Australia ; a stay at the Gold Diggings ; an expedition through Gippsland, across the Australian Alps, in the course of which death from starvation was close upon him ; a cruise in the Pacific, ending in a holiday on the Hawaiian Islands ; and then, at last, back to England. Later came less venturesome travel on the continent of Europe ; long residencies in Italy, France, and Germany ; two visits to America. For one who understood how to use it, such journeyman life was of the highest value.

As he has proved, this journeyman did know how to use it. On his return to England from the antipodes, he formed a friendship with Dante Gabriel Rossetti which brought him speedily into intimate association with the most interesting group of literary men that London has known since the early years of the century. His appreciative feeling for his surroundings was shown later in his Life of Rossetti ; while the *developing effect of these surroundings upon his critical faculty was exhibited in his scholarly editorial work—notably in his Canterbury Poets Series—and to a still more marked degree in his Life of Heine : a critical study of the first value, outranking all else—not even excepting his Life of Browning—that as yet he has accomplished in prose.*

By Mr. Sharp's own election (since, with a cruelty unmerited, he has disowned almost all of his earlier work in verse) his standing as a poet practically will be rated by the poems which are collected within this volume.   Certainly, he need not fear the result.   The quantity is small, but the qualities are rare, and of a rare excellence. I say "qualities," as though the writings of two poets were gathered here ; and, in truth, the widely differing sorts of poetry which are assembled within these covers very well might pass for the utterances of two men of different races and widely sundered climes.   Here, joined but not blended, is the poetry of the South and of the North. It is an inversion of that curious process by which the waters of the White and Blue rivers, whereof the Nile is made, flowing out from separate sources, journey on together in the same channel for a long while without mingling. In this case, the two streams of verse come from the same source—yet instantly are so distinct and separate that the most acutely critical of observers would not be likely to refer them to a common origin.

But in each of the forms of poetic expression which he employs—in the ballad measure, and in the more subtle arrangement of words by which rhythm is achieved without rhyme—this Poet has hereditary rights; for both of these forms come to him by descent from his remote progenitors the Scottish bards. His ballad making, indeed, is of so admirable a quality—not merely in its versification, but in its nice choice and development of theme—that we must try far back into the centuries, to the eerie creations of those same Scottish singers, to find its parallel. For this Poet, like those of the elder day, has drawn his inspiration direct from local legend and from rugged nature and has clothed his thoughts in terse, aggressive words—wherefore his writing has little in common with the modern poesy (as its contrivers fitly call it) which abounds in rounded syllables and echoes daintily the airs and graces of the town. His ballads are not mere masses of rhymes dexterously fitted together : they are poems with living souls.

I cannot fancy a stronger literary contrast than is found in turning from these stern utterances to the soft Sospiri di Roma ; from the strange shadows lit by vivid flashes from supernatural fires of the mysterious North to the glowing and generously open splendour of the South. It seems entirely in keeping with the abrupt transition that the restraint of rhyme

*should be left behind and that this poetry of the South
should be controlled only by a rhythm as lithe, as subtly
illusive, and as evanescent as is the rhythm of the
southern wind. This irregular, unrhymed measure is
a very primitive method. So sang of old our Poet's
own Gaelic minstrels ; so sing to-day the gentle savages
of the South Sea among whom for a while he sojourned.
For the thought which he wished to convey he could not
have employed a more fitting vehicle. An English critic
has observed that " when irregular measures do achieve
a triumph they leave upon us the priceless impression
of spontaneity and sincerity " ; and the artistic reason
why the Sospiri di Roma were shaped in an unusual
form is found in the fact that spontaneity and sincerity
were the qualities supremely necessary to the adequate
development of the Poet's selected themes. His employ-
ment of what Monkhouse has termed " poetry in solu-
tion" is not the resource of a careless or incapable
writer who cannot work within the precise limitations
of ordinary measures ; it is the deliberate choice of
a dangerously facile method by one who is justified in
using it because his hand is strong enough for its
control.*

*That a new singer should be born into the world is
not, after all, a very wonderful matter ; for it is a
blessed truth that such creations of genius ever are
coming forward newly for the pleasure and comfort of*

mankind. But, with submission, I do hold to be remarkable this birth of a singer who sings so excellently in such strangely separate keys ; this merging of two distinct patents of poetic nobility in a single fortunate heir.

Thomas A. Janvier.

New York, April 7, 1892.

FLOWER O' THE VINE

CONTENTS

OF THE NORTH:

ROMANTIC BALLADS
AND
POEMS OF PHANTASY

NOTE

(*Michael the Scot : fl.* circa 1250.) Variants of the Michael Scott legends still exist in parts of the Scottish Southlands: betwixt Tweed and Forth, mainly in the remote districts of the shires of Selkirk, Peebles, and Roxburgh; and, north of the Forth, here and there along the Fife coast. The most common is that which relates to the magician's power of changing into an animal anyone who crossed him; and it is upon this that Part I. of the following ballad turns. That also is current which relates how Michael the Scot could win the soul from the body of any woman whom he loved. There are several versions of this uncanny kind of wooing: sometimes Michael Scott is said to have seduced the spirit from its tranced tenement, only to find himself eluded after all; sometimes the maiden, unable to resist his spell, comes to him, but over the battlements, and so is killed; again, just as she is about to yield she calls on Christ, and only a phantasmal image of her goes forth, though in the struggle her mortal body perishes (it was upon this version that Rossetti intended to write a poem; his prose outline of it is given in his Collected Works); or, yet again, she comes at her wizard-lover's signal, but when he would embrace her a cross of fire intervenes, and, to save himself from sudden hell-flames which arise, he has perforce to bid her return in safety. I have in Part II. treated Michael Scott's allurement of Margaret's soul not wholly accordantly with any legendary account, yet in superficial conformity with that which most appealed to my imagination. Part III. is in treatment entirely imaginary, although, of course, the germinal idea —that of encountering at the point of death one's own soul—is both old and widespread. The Doppelgänger idea is a most impressive one in its crudest guise, and I have endeavoured to heighten its imaginative effect by making Michael Scott pronounce unwittingly a dreadful doom upon his own soul.

ROMANTIC BALLADS

THE WEIRD OF MICHAEL SCOTT

THE wild wind moaned: fast waned the light:
Dense cloud-wrack gloomed the front of night :
The moorland cries were cries of pain :
Green, red, or broad and glaring white
The lightnings flashed athwart the main.

The sound and fury of the waves,
Upon the rocks, among the caves,
Boomed inland from the thunderous strand :
Mayhap the dead heard in their graves
The tumult fill the hollow land.

With savage pebbly rush and roar
The billows swept the echoing shore
In clouds of spume and swirling spray :
The wild wings of the tempest bore
The salt rime to the Haunted Brae.

Upon the Haunted Brae (where none
Would linger in the noontide sun)
Michael the Wizard rode apace :
Wildly he rode where all men shun,
With madness gleaming on his face.

Loud, loud he laugh'd whene'er he saw
The lightnings split on Lammer-Law,
" *'Blood, bride, and bier,' the auld rune saith*
Hell's wind tae me ae nicht sall blaw,
The nicht I ride unto my death !"

Across the Haunted Brae he fled,
And mock'd and jeer'd the shuddering dead ,
Wan white the horse that he bestrode,
The fire-flaughts stricken as it sped
Flashed thro' the black mirk of the road.

And ever as his race he ran,
A shade pursued the fleeing man,
A white and ghastly shade it was ;
" Like saut sea-spray across wet san'
Or wind abune the moonlit grass !—

" Like saut sea-spray it follows me,
Or wind o'er grass—so fast's I flee :
In vain I shout, and laugh, and call—
The thing betwixt me and the sea
God kens it is my ain lost saul !"

Down, down the Haunted Brae, and past
The verge of precipices vast
And eyries where the eagles screech ;
By great pines swaying in the blast,
Through woods of moaning larch and beech ;

On, on by moorland glen and stream,
Past lonely lochs where ospreys scream,
Past marsh-lands where no sound is heard,
The rider and his white horse gleam,
And, aye behind, that dreadful third.

Wild and more wild the wild wind blew,
But Michael Scott the rein ne'er drew :
Loud and more loud his laughter shrill,
His wild and mocking laughter, grew,
In dreadful cries 'twixt hill and hill.

At last the great high road he gained,
And now with whip and voice he strained
To swifter flight the gleaming mare ;
Afar ahead the fierce sleet rained
Upon the ruin'd House of Stair.

Then Michael Scott laughed long and loud
"Whan shone the mune ahint yon cloud
I kent the Towers that saw my birth—
Lang, lang, sall wait my cauld grey shroud,
Lang cauld and weet my bed o' earth ! "

But as by Stair he rode full speed
His horse began to pant and bleed :
"Win hame, win hame, my bonnie mare,
Win hame if thou would'st rest and feed,
Win hame, we're nigh the House of Stair !"

But with a shrill heart-bursten yell
The white horse stumbled, plunged, and fell,
And loud a summoning voice arose,
"Is't White-Horse Death that rides frae Hell,
Or Michael Scott that hereby goes?"

"Ah, Lord of Stair, I ken ye weel !
Avaunt, or I your saul sall steal,
An' send ye howling through the wood
A wild man-wolf—aye, ye maun reel
An' cry upon your Holy Rood !"

Swift swept the sword within the shade,
Swift was the flash the blue steel made,
Swift was the downward stroke and rash—
But, as though levin-struck, the blade
Fell splintered earthward with a crash.

With frantic eyes Lord Stair out-peered
Where Michael Scott laughed loud and jeered :—
"Forth fare ye now, ye've gat lang room !
Ah, by my saul thou'lt dree thy weird !
Begone, were-wolf, till the day o' doom !"

A shrill scream pierced the lonely place ;
A dreadful change came o'er the face ;
The head, with bristled hair, swung low ;
Michael the Wizard turned and fled
And laughed a mocking laugh of woe.

And through the wood there stole and crept,
And through the wood there raced and leapt,
A thing in semblance of a man ;
An awful look its wild eyes kept
As howling through the night it ran.

PART II

ATHWART the wan bleak moonlit waste,
With staring eyes, in frantic haste,
With thin locks back-blown by the wind,
A grey gaunt haggard figure raced
And moaned the thing that sped behind.

It followed him, afar or near :
In wrath he curs'd ; he shrieked in fear ;
But ever more it followed him :
Oftimes he stopp'd, to stoop, to peer,
To front the following phantom grim.

Naught would he see ; in vain would list
For wing-like sound or feet that hissed
As wind-blown snow upon the ice ;
The grey thing vanished like a mist,
Or like the smoke of sacrifice :

"Come forth beyont the mirk," his cry,
"For I maun live or I maun die,
But na, na mair I'll suffer baith !"
Then, with a shriek, would onward fly :
And, swift behind, his following wraith.

Michael the Wizard sped across
The peat and bracken o' the moss:
He heard the muir-wind rise and fall,
And laughed to see the birk-boughs toss
An' the stealthy shadows leap or crawl.

When white St. Monan's Water streamed
For leagues athwart the muir, and gleamed
With phosphorescent marish-fires,
With wild and sudden joy he screamed,
For scarce a mile was Kevan-Byres—

Sweet Kevan-Byres, dear Kevan-Byres,
That oft of old was thronged with squires
And joyous damsels blithe and gay :
Alas, alas for Kevan-Byres
That now is cold and grey.

There in her bed on linen sheet
With white soft limbs and love-dreams sweet
Fair Margaret o' the Byres would be :
(Ah, when he'd lain and kissed her feet
Had she not laughed in mockery !)

Aye, she had laughed, for what reck'd she
O' a' the powers of Wizardie !
" Win up, win up, guid Michael Scott,
For ye sall ne'er win boon o' me,
By plea, or sword, or spell, God wot !"

Aye, these the words that she had said :
These were the words that as he fled
Michael the Wizard muttered o'er—
"My Margaret, bow your bonnie head,
For ye sall never flout me more !"

Swiftly he raced, with gleaming eyes,
And wild, strange, sobbing, panting cries,
Dire, dire, and fell his frantic mood ;
Until he gained St. Monan's Rise
Whereon the House of Kevan stood.

There looked he long and fixed his gaze
Upon a room where in past days
His very soul had pled love's boon :
Lit was it now with the wan rays
Flick-flickering from the cloud-girt moon.

"Come forth, May Margaret, come, my heart !
For thou and I nae mair sall part—
Come forth, I bid, though Christ himsel'
My bitter love should strive to thwart,
For I have a' the powers o' Hell !"

What was the white wan thing that came
And lean'd from out the window-frame,
Waving wild arms against the sky?
What was the hollow echoing name,
What was the thin despairing cry?

Adown the long and dusky stair,
Across the courtyard bleak and bare,
Swift past the gate, and out upon
The whistling, moaning, midnight air—
What is't that Michael Scott has won?

Across the moat it seems to flee,
It speeds across the windy lea,
And through the ruin'd abbey-arch;
Now like a mist all waveringly
It stands beneath a lonely larch.

"Come, Margaret, my Margaret,
Ye see my vows I ne'er forget:
Come win wi' me across the waste—
Lang, lang I've wandered cauld and wet,
An' now thy sweet warm lips would taste!"

But as a whirling drift of snow,
Or flying foam the sea-winds blow,
Or smoke swept thin before a gale,
It flew across the waste—and oh
'Twas Margaret's voice in that long wail!

Swift as the hound upon the deer,
Swift as the stag when nigh the mere,
Michael the Wizard followed fast—
What though May Margaret fled in fear,
She should be his, be his, at last!—

O'er broom and whin and bracken high,
Where the peat bog lay gloomily,
Where sullenly the bittern boomed
And startled curlews swept the sky,
Until St. Monan's Water loomed !

" The cauld wet water sall na be
The bride-bed for my love and me—
For now upon St. Monan's shore
May Margaret her love sall gie
To him she mocked and jeered of yore !"

Was that a heron in its flight ?
Was that a mere-mist wan and white ?
What thing from lonely kirkyard grave ?
Forlorn it trails athwart the night
With arms that writhe and wring and wave !

Deep down within the mere it sank,
Among the slimy reeds and rank,
And all the leagues-long loch was bare—
One vast, grey, moonlit, lifeless blank
Beneath a silent waste of air.

" O God, O God ! her soul it is !
Christ's saved her frae my blasting kiss !
Her soul frae out her body drawn,
The body I maun have for bliss !
O body dead and spirit gaun !"

Hours long o'er Monan's wave he stared.
The fire-flaughts flashed and gleamed and glared,
The death-lights o' the lonely place :
And aye, dead-still, he watch'd, till flared
The sunrise on his haggard face.

Full well he knew that with its fires
Loud was the tumult 'mong the squires,
And fierce the bitter pain of all
Where stark and stiff in Kevan-Byres
May Margaret lay beneath her pall.

Then once he laughed, and twice, and thrice,
Though deep within his hollow eyes
Dull-gleamed a light of fell despair.
Around, Earth grew a Paradise
In the sweet golden morning air.

Slowly he rose at last, and swift
One gaunt and frantic arm did lift
And curs'd God in his heav'n o'erhead :
Then, like a lonely cloud adrift,
Far from St. Monan's wave he fled.

PART III

ALL day the curlew wailed and screamed,
All day the cushat crooned and dreamed,
All day the sweet muir-wind blew free :
Beyond the grassy knowes far gleamed
The splendour of the singing sea.

Above the myriad gorse and broom
And miles of golden kingcup-bloom
The larks and yellowhammers sang :
Where the scaur cast an hour-long gloom
The lintie's falling notes out-rang.

Oft as he wandered to and fro—
As idly as the foam-bells flow
Hither and thither on the deep—
Michael the Wizard's face would grow
From death to life, and he would weep—

Weep, weep hot tears of bitter pain
For what might never be again :
Yet even as he wept his face
Would gleam with mockery insane.
With laughter fierce on would he race,

Screaming a wild and savage cry,
Till awed to silence by the sky
Unfathomable, vast, serene:
Then would he wayfare silently
With hush'd and furtive mein.

At times he watch'd the white clouds sail
Across the wastes of azure pale ;
Or oft would haunt some moorland pool
Fringed round with thyme and fragrant gale
And canna-tufts of snow-white wool.

Long in its depths would Michael stare,
As though some secret thing lay there :
Mayhap the moving water made
A gloom where crouched a Kelpie fair
With death-eyes gleaming through the shade.

Then on with weary listless feet
He fared afar, until the sweet
Cool sound of mountain brooks drew nigh,
And loud he heard the strayed lambs bleat
And the white ewes responsive cry.

High up among the hills full clear
He heard the belling of the deer
Amid the corries where they browsed,
And, where the peaks rose gaunt and sheer,
Fierce swirling echoes eagle-roused.

He watched the kestrel wheel and sweep,
He watched the dun fox glide and creep,
He heard the whaup's long-echoing call,
Watched in the stream the brown trout leap
And the grilse spring the waterfall.

Along the slopes the grouse-cock whirred;
The grey-blue heron scarcely stirred
Amid the mossed grey tarn-side stones:
The burns gurg-gurgled through the yird
Their sweet clear bubbling undertones.

Above the tarn the dragon-fly
Shot like a flashing arrow by ;
Vague in a moving shifting haze
The gnat-clouds sank or soared on high
And danced their wild aërial maze.

As the day waned he heard afar
The hawking fern-owl's dissonant jar
Disturb the silence of the hill :
The gloaming came : star after star
He watched the skiey spaces fill.

But as the darkness grew and made
Forest and mountain one vast shade,
Michael the Wizard moaned in dread—
A long white moonbeam like a blade
Swept after him where'er he fled.

Swiftly he leapt o'er rock and root,
Swift o'er the fern his flying foot,
But swifter still the white moonbeam :
Wild was the grey-owl's dismal hoot,
But wilder still his maniac scream.

Once in his flight he paused to hear
A hollow shriek that echoed near :—
The louder were his dreadful cries,
The louder rang adown the sheer
Gaunt cliffs the echoing replies.

As though a hunted wolf, he raced
To the lone woods across the waste
Steep granite slopes of Crammond-Low—
The haunted forest where none faced
The terror that no man might know.

Betwixt the mountains and the sea
Dark leagues of pine stood solemnly,
Voiceful with grim and hollow song,
Save when each tempest-stricken tree
A savage tumult would prolong.

Beneath the dark funereal plumes, ·
Slow waving to and fro—death-blooms
Within the void dim wood of death—
Oft shuddering at the fearful glooms
Sped Michael Scott with failing breath.

Once, as he passed a dreary place,
Between two trees he saw a face—
A white face staring at his own :
A weird strange cry he gave for grace,
And heard an echoing moan.

" Whate'er you be, O thing that hides
Among the trees—O thing that bides
In yonder moving mass o' shade
Come forth tae me !"—wan Michael glides
Swift, as he speaks, athwart the glade :

"Whate'er you be, I fear ye nought !
Michael the Wizard has na fought
Wi' men and demons year by year
To shirk ae thing he has na sought
Or blanch wi' any mortal fear !"

But not a sound thrilled thro' the air—
Not even a she-fox in her lair
Or brooding bird made any stir—
All was as still and blank and bare
As is a vaulted sepulchre.

Then awe, and fear, and wild dismay
O'ercame mad Michael, ashy grey,
With eyes as of one newly dead :
"If wi' my sword I canna slay,
Thou'lt dree my weird when it is said !

" Whate'er you be, man, beast, or sprite,
I wind ye round wi' a sheet o' light—
Aye, round and round your burning frame
I cast by spell o' wizard might
A fierce undying sheet of flame !"

Swift as he spoke a thing sprang out,
A man-like thing, all hemmed about
With blazing blasting burning fire !
The wind swoop'd wi' a demon-shout
And whirled the red flame higher and higher !

And as, appalled, wan Michael stood
The flying flaughts swift fired the wood;
And even as he shook and stared
The gaunt pines turned the hue of blood
And all the waving branches flared.

Then with wild leaps the accursëd thing
Drew ever nigher : with a spring
Michael escaped its fiery clasp,
Although he felt the fierce flame sting
And all the horror of its grasp.

Swift as an arrow far he fled,
But swifter still the flames o'erhead
Rushed o'er the waving sea of pines,
And hollow noises crashed and sped
Like splitting blasts in ruin'd mines.

A burning league—leagues, leagues of fire
Arose behind, and ever higher
The flying semi-circle came :
And aye beyond this dreadful pyre
There leapt a man-like thing in flame.

.

With awful scream doom'd Michael saw
The flying furnace reach Black-Law :
" ' *Blood, bride, and bier,' the auld rune saith,*
Hell's wind tae me ae nicht sall blaw,
The nicht I ride unto my death!

" *The blood of Stair is round me now:*
My bride can laugh to scorn my vow :
My bier, my bier, ah sall it be
Wi' a crown o' fire around my brow
Or deep within the cauld saut sea!"

Like lightning, over Black-Law's slope
Michael fled swift with sudden hope :
What though the forest roared behind—
He yet might gain the cliff and grope
For where the sheep-paths twist and wind.

The air was like a furnace-blast
And all the dome of heaven one vast
Expanse of flame and fiery wings :
To the cliff's edge, ere all be past,
With shriek on shriek lost Michael springs.

But none can hear his bitter call,
None, none can see him sway and fall—
Yea, one there is that shrills his name !
"O God, it is my ain lost saul
That I hae girt wi' deathless flame !"

With waving arms and dreadful cries
He cowers beneath those glaring eyes—
But all in vain—in vain—in vain !
His own soul clasps him as its prize
And scorches death upon his brain.

Body and soul together swing
Adown the night until they fling
The hissing sea-spray far and wide :
At morn the fresh sea-wind will bring
A black corpse tossing on the tide.

Allan, son of Allan, Chief of the Colquhouns, had wooed and won Adair, daughter of Malcolm McDiarmid ; but on the day the nuptials were to have taken place she was carried off in willing flight by MacDonald of the Isles. Allan pursued with twenty of Lord Malcolm's men, but arrived on the lonely Argyll sea-board only an hour too late, MacDonald having just sailed in triumph to his western isles. Allan for a time lost his reason, but in the autumn again regained his former vigour, and it was shortly after this time, in the first month of the New Year, that a message came at last from MacDonald offering to privily meet the man he had wronged, and fight out their quarrel alone.

The ballad opens on the eve of this duel. Allan, nigh upon the appointed meeting-place on a lonely hill-side, waits the fixt hour at the hut of one known as the Witch of Dunmore. She forsees the fatal result of the duel to her clansman as well as to his foe, and strives to dissuade him from the combat—recalling her past experiences to him and mentioning signs and portents, hoping thus to convince him of the truth of her vision.

THE SON OF ALLAN

" THE wind soughs weird through the moaning pines,
The icy moon through the fierce frost shines,
The steel-blue stars are baleful signs,
                    Son of Allan ! "
      " *The wind may blow to its last faint breath,*
      Ere I turn aside from the shadow of death ! "

" My dreams come true: thou knowest my laugh
Hath split the mountain-shepherd's staff,
Hath blown the ripe grain into chaff—
                    Son of Allan ! "
      " *Your curse may come and your curse may go—*
      My soul must dree some other woe ! "

" When New Year came with gusty moan
I lay forgot, accurst, alone—
But I saw the scroll of your life as my own,
                    Son of Allan ! "
      " *God knows if Hell or Heaven's my life,*
      To-night is hoarse with the sound of strife ! "

" And I saw you ride one sweet May morn,
When the missel-thrush sang on the flowering thorn—
O better if you had ne'er been born,
                Son of Allan !"
    " *I would that God had strangled my soul—*
    But living, to-night I seek one goal !"

" And I saw you ride by the brown-stoned burn,
And your horse's hooves the flag-flowers spurn—
O turn ye now, while yet ye can turn,
                Son of Allan !"
    " *The fierce tides ebb from the sea-drench'd shore,*
    But I turn not now till one thing's o'er !"

" And I saw you leave the speckled stream
Where the moor-hen clucks and the plovers scream,
And ride with your eyes in a far-off dream,
                Son of Allan !"
    " *Long weeks ago I dreamt, and now*
    The awakening nears my fever'd brow !"

" And I saw you leave the woods apace
And seek Dunallan's grassy ways,
With a golden glory on your face,
                Son of Allan !"
    " *A thousand years ago I sought*
    My love's cruel death, and knew it not !"

" And I saw you choose a ready stall,
And leave your horse by the castle wall,
And loudly for the henchman call,
          Son of Allan ! "
   " No more on men or maids I call—
   I or he this night shall fall ! "

" And I saw you leap the deer-skinned stair,
And I saw you kiss the golden hair
And the sweet red lips of Lady Adair,
          Son of Allan ! "
   " I kissed her lips—each kiss a coal
   That burns and flames within my soul ! "

" And I heard you say, ' My love, my dear,
How speed the maids with the bridal gear? '
And then you whispered in her ear,
          Son of Allan ! "
   " I whispered then—but one shall know
   No whispers soon when he lies low ! "

" And I saw them fill the one great room,
Where the sword-scarred pennons waved in gloom,
With a golden dish for every plume,
          Son of Allan ! "
   " White plumes may flaunt, white plumes may wave!
   White swords shall this night carve a grave ! "

" And I saw the wine-cups filled brim-high,
And joy shine bright in your bonnie blue eye
As ' Lady Adair ' was your toasting cry,
> Son of Allan!"
> *" I hear no more the wine-cups clash,—*
> *I hear the gurgling red blood splash!"*

" And I heard Lord Malcolm call out loud
For his daughter fair,—and I saw a bowed
Old henchman quake 'mid the servile crowd,
> Son of Allan!"
> *" Let traitors sweat with sudden fright!*
> *Goa's wrath disturbs the world to-night!"*

" But as sleet rings fierce on a wind-beat grange,
His words fell swift, and stinging, and strange,—
Lord Malcolm's smile had an awful change,
> Son of Allan!"
> *" God's smile was lost in a deep dark frown—*
> *But one of twain shall this night fall down!"*

" And I saw thy face wax flushed, then pale,
And thy lips grow blue like black-ice hail,
With eyes on fire with the soul's fierce bale,
> Son of Allan!"
> *" Pale, pale I was with my soul's dread,—*
> *But one this night shall lie full red!"*

" And 1 heard Lord Malcolm cry ' To horse!
MacDonald has swooped with the falcon's force,
But we'll catch them both ere they end their course,
Son of Allan!'"
" The hawk may swoop, and the dove may fly,
But the hawk for the dove this night shall die! "

" And I saw thee haste, and mount, and away
With twenty men by thy side that day,
And thy face was like the gloaming grey,
Son of Allan!"
" Long, long ago the sun shone bright,—
But since that day black mirk o' night! "

" And I saw thee ride through the brief chill dark,
Till dawn awakened each sinless lark,
And the hills re-echoed the sheep-dog's bark,
Son of Allan!"
" Ah ! long ago sweet morns were fair,—
Now blood seems dropping everywhere! "

"Till the horses tramped in the blazing noon,
And the cuckoo called farewell to June,
And the blackbird sang a blithe glad tune,
Son of Allan!"
" Ah ! once I knew that sweet birds sang—
I hear nought now but steel's harsh clang !

" And, Son of Allan, ere swart night fell,
I heard Lord Malcolm's savage yell,
And saw thy face in the shadow of hell,
              Son of Allan!"
    " *Hope died upon that cursèd strand—*
    But to-night we meet, each sword in hand! "

" For the horses plashed on the wave-washed shore,
And MacDonald had sailed an hour before:
Thy bride to his isles the chieftain bore,
              Son of Allan!"
    " *My bride! my bride! no bride have I—*
    But a bridegroom this night shall fall and die! "

" And I saw thee fall like one struck dead;
And they made for thee a pine-branch bed—
And thus-wise with thee home they sped,
              Son of Allan!"
    " *O would to God I had met him where*
    He kissed and fondled his Lady Adair! "

" And I saw the fever burn and flame
Like fire through all thy tortured frame,
And ever shrill'dst thou one fair name,
              Son of Allan!"
    " *O false, false heart of Lady Adair,*
    Whose corpse behold you cold and bare? "

" Not till the autumn's purple days
Did thine eyes lose their empty gaze—
Then Reason came in one sharp blaze,
        Son of Allan!"
   " *O madness comes and madness goes,*
    But the slain corpse no madness knows! "

" Then word was brought MacDonald sent—
He bade you rest no more content
With dreams of anguish impotent,
        Son of Allan!"
   " *No dreams I dream! one thing I know,*
    This night a soul to hell doth go! "

" And now beneath the New Year moon
He rides to grant your final boon—
And neither shall see Spring wed to June,
        Son of Allan!"
   " *Sweet Junes may bloom, and Junes may blow,*
    But a soul this night shall taste of woe! "

" He grasps the hilt of his waist-band knife,
And he smiles as he thinks of his laughing wife,
And his blood leaps hard as a steed's for strife,
        Son of Allan!"
   " *Aye! loud she may laugh, and loud may he,*
    But his eyes shall gladden no more at the sea! "

" My dreams come true: upon my bed
Last night I dreamt I saw o'erhead
A darkness fold thee, and leave thee dead,
   Son of Allan!"
 " *The mirk you saw is light to what*
  Will gather when he and I have fought!"

" Stop, stop!" (the Witch of Dunmore calls)
"I see in vision the man who falls:
A cloud of blood my sight appals,
   Son of Allan!"
 " *I wait no more for thy blind words—*
  No words this night but gleaming swords!"

" The wind soughs weird through the moaning pines,
The icy moon through the fierce frost shines,
The steel-blue stars are baleful signs,
   Son of Allan!"
 " *The wind may blow to its last faint breath—*
  Cross swords, cross swords, for life or death!"

" Back bloody swords!   Forbear, forbear!
Lord Allan see, thy wraith is there—
The stars gleam through its shadow-hair,
   O son of Allan!"
 " *O dripping sword, spring, lunge, and sweep!*
  O thirsting sword, drink deep, drink deep!"

MAD MADGE O' CREE

HITHER and thither, to and fro,
    She wander'd o'er the bleak hill-sides;
She watch'd the wild Sound toss and flow,
    And the water-kelpies lead the tides.

She heard the wind upon the hill
    Or wailing wild across the muir,
And answered it with laughter shrill
    And mocked its eldritch lure.

Within the running stream she heard
    A music such as none may hear;
The voice of every beast and bird
    Had meaning for her ear.

" What seek ye thus, fair Margery?
    Ye know your Ranald's dead:
Win hame, my bonnie lass, wi' me,
    Win hame to hearth and bed !"

. " Hark ! hear ye not the corbie call—
  It shrills, *Come owre the glen,*
  For Ranald standeth fair and tall
    Amid his shadow-men ! "

" ' His shadow-men,' O Margery !
  'Tis of the dead ye speak:
Syne they are in the saut deep sea
  What gars ye phantoms seek ? "

" Hark, hear ye not the curlew wail
  May Margery mak haste,
For Ranald wanders sad and pale
  About the lonely waste."

" O Margery, what is't ye say:
  Your Ranald's dead and drowned.
Neither by night, neither by day,
  Sall your fair love be found."

" He is not dead, for I hae seen
  His bonnie gowden hair:
Within his arms I've claspit been,
  An' I have dreamit there:

" Last night I stood by green Craigmore
  And watch'd the foaming tide:
And there across the moonlit shore
  A shadow sought my side.

" But when he kissed me soft and sweet,
    And faintly ca'd tae me,
I rose an' took his hand an' fleet
    We sought the Caves o' Cree.

" Ah, there we kissed, my love and I:
    An' there sad songs he sang
O' how dead men drift wearily
    'Mid sea-wrack lank and lang.

" And once my wan love whisper'd low
    How 'mid the sea-weeds deep,
As but yestreen he drifted slow,
    He saw me lying asleep—

" Aye sound in sleep beneath the wave
    Wi' shells an' sea-things there,
An' as the tide swept o'er my grave
    . It stirred like weed my hair:

" In vain, ah, all in vain, he tried
    To reach an' clasp my hand,
To lay his body by my side
    Upon that shell-strewn strand.

" But ah, within the Caves o' Cree
    He kissed my lips full fain—
Ay, by the hollow booming sea
    We'll meet, my love, again."

That night again fair Margery
 In Cree-Caves slept full sound,
And by her side lay lovingly
 The wan wraith of the drowned.

O what is yon toss-tossing there
 Where a' the white gulls fly:
Is yon gold weed or golden hair
 The waves swirl merrily?

O what is yon white shape that slips
 Among the lapsing seas:
Pale, pale the rose-red of the lips
 Whereo'er the spindrift flees.

What bears the tide unto the strand
 Where the drown'd seaman lies?
A waving arm, a hollow hand,
 And face with death-dimmed eyes.

The tide uplifts them, leaves them where
 Each first knew love beside the sea:
Bound each to each with yellow hair
 Within the Caves o' Cree.

THE DEITH-TIDE

" *Wi' a risin' win',*
  An' a flowin' tide,
    There's a deith tae be;
  When the win' gaes back
  An' the tide's at the slack,
    There's a spirit free."
—FRAGMENT OF A HIGHLAND FOLKSONG.

THE weet saut wind is blawing
Upon the misty shore:
And like a stormy snawing
The deid go streaming o'er:—

The wan drown'd deid sail wildly
Frae out each drumly wave:
It's O and O for the weary sea
And O for a quiet grave.

" Whose voice is that is calling
Amid the deid-wrack there,
What saut tears these aye falling
Upon my rain-weet hair?

" What white thing blawing, blawing
Before the moaning gale,
The grey thing 'mid the snawing,
The white thing 'mid the hail? "

The wan drown'd deid sail wildly
Forth frae each sullen wave:
It's O and O for the weary sea
And O for a quiet grave.

" O wha be ye that's mournin'
Down by the saut sea-shore—
Mournin', mournin', mournin'
Alang the saut sea-shore:

" O weel I ken my dearie,
My dear love lost lang-syne:
O weep nae mair my dearie
Your tears o' bitter brine:

" The weet saut win' is falling,
An' hear ye not the tide,
The deith-tide calling, calling?
O come wi' me, my bride !

" O come wi' me, my marrow,
Ye'll sleep love's sleep at last,
No in a cauld bed narrow
But swirlin' on the blast—

" O come wi' me my ain ain Jean—
What gars ye grow sae chill ? "
" O I fear your hollow burnin' een,
An' your voice sae thin an' shrill ! "

" O come wi' me my marrow,
Sae sweet sall be your sleep,
No in a cauld bed narrow
But in the swayin' deep."

> The wan drown'd deid sail wildly
> Frae back the weary land:
> It's O and O for the saut deep sea
> Ayont the barren strand.

" O weel my soul is flyin'
Abune the faem wi' thee:
My bodie white, cauld, cauld is lyin'
Beside the gurly sea:

" O gie tae me your shadowy han'
An' swift your phantom-kiss,
It's drear, sae drear, within the mirk
Here where the white waves hiss ! "

> The wan drown'd deid sail wildly
> Frae back the weary land;
> It's O and O for the saut deep sea
> Ayont the barren strand.

THE LAST VOYAGE OF KEIR THE MONK

("*And the Joy of the World hath many names; and none knoweth her
save they be born again before they die.*"   H. P. Siwäarmill.)

Singing his song of sunrise
  Keir launched his island-boat:
Singing his song of sunrise
  He soon was far afloat.

He smiled to see the wavelets
  Leap in the dancing shine,
The glad sea far and wide
  Like unto golden wine.

Against the deep blue hollow
  Of the unfathom'd sky,
Like blown white flowers the seamews
  Went sailing, drifting, by.

Along the vague blue mainland,
  Among the perilous shoals,
The fishing-smacks went quietly
  As dying souls.

He heard the island brethren
   Singing the matin hymn;
For one brief moment only
   His eager eyes were dim.

Singing his song of sunrise,
   Keir bade the monks farewell:
" For ye are bound for heaven, ye think,
   And I'm adrift for hell."

" O beautiful, O beautiful,
   The world is now become:
I am no longer blind and deaf,
   No longer dumb:

" O beautiful, O beautiful "
   (Thus Keir the monk did sing)
" The glory of the laughing world,
   The virgin Spring ! "

And ever as he sang he rowed
   And made the wavelets leap:
" I am as one who wakens late
   From dark bewildered sleep !

" O beautiful, O beautiful
   The lovely splashing sea:
The yellow sands of Aberdour,
   And branches waving free—

" Branches, green branches
  That beckon me to follow
Down to where the forest falls
  Into a little hollow !

" Who singeth there so lowly
  By moonshine or at noon:
Singing a low song sweetly
  To an old forgotten tune ?

" An' if she be no maiden
  Begot as women are.
More lovely is the elfin-maid
  Who dwells afar.

" She dwells deep in the woodlands,
  Or where the hill tarns gleam,
Or where the upland pastures
  Rise from valleys of dream.

" O beautiful, O beautiful
  Is she my mystic fay:
The lovely pathos of the night,
  The glory of the day—

" The glory of the day is hers,
  The pathos of the night:
She hath won me by her golden hair,
  Her eyes of shadowy light.

"She walks the woods of Aberdour:
    Her song is heard afar:
For she an elfin-maiden is,
    And not as women are.

"In woods of Aberdour,
    Or by the yellow sands,
She looks into my eyes and laughs,
    And takes me by the hands.

"If she hath won my perished soul
    And I am lost for aye—
Sweet is my loss, O sweet my loss,
    And brief at best my day."

.   .   .   .   .   .

They found them In the woods at dusk,
    Lured by the phantom song:
They bound them each to each, and haled
    The two lost souls along.

They took them to the moonlit strand
    Of lonely Aberdour:
And there they dug within the sand
    A narrow bridal bower.

"Soft shall ye lie, O Keir:" they cried:
    "Loud may ye call at last,
For the only change for ye shall be
    The wind o' hell's hot blast,"

And they tramped the loose sand o'er their heads,
   And sang their monkish hymn,
And joyed to know their brother's cup
   Was fillëd to the brim.

But as they trampled wi' their feet
   And sang their monkish hymn,
A shimmering mist cam' out o' the sea
   And wavered white and dim.

" The phantom-woman will na bide—
   God thwart her demon-saul ! "
So cried the Prior in fear—and then
   Keir stood amidst them all.

" O art thou but an awfu' thing
   Out of the grave that's come:
O art thou Keir the monk that lies
   White and cold and numb ? "

" I am Keir the monk, as ye know well,"
   But he laughed low as he spake:
" I have had a long sweet sleep, and now
   Once more I wake."   .

They seized him by his bloody hair
   Still damp with his wet grave,
And dragged him down and flung him far
   Into the salt deep wave.

But when they reached the Holy Isle
    Keir walked upon the shore:
" Thy soul is lost, O Keir ! " they cried:
    He laughed: " For Evermore."

All night he walked the Holy Isle,
    And some one with him there:
None knoweth what the white thing was
    With the veil of golden hair.

But ere the dawn Keir sought his cell
    And wrote upon the wall:
" *God said*, REJOICE: *and who was I*
    To mumble at the call ! "

Singing his song of sunrise,
    Keir launched his island-boat :
Singing his song of sunrise
    He soon was far afloat.

Singing his song of sunrise
    They heard him bid farewell:—
" For I am bound for heaven, I wist,
    And ye are still in hell."

POEMS OF PHANTASY

POEMS OF PHANTASY

PHANTASY

Riding o'er a lonely plain
I came unto a wood—
Straying I met, in dreamful mood,
A damsel singing a low strain,
All ye who love me love in vain!

Her song it seeméd far away,
But oh her kiss was sweet:
She led me to some green retreat,
And there within her arms I lay
The livelong day.

All ye who love me love in vain—
I kissed her wistful face
But found a leaf-strewn space
Alone, and far I heard her strain,
All ye who love me love in vain!

I seek the wood in twilit hours—
    At times I hear her sing;
    At times her white arms round me cling:
She leads me into magic bow'rs
And sings and wreaths me wilding flow'rs.

Her eyes are tears, and pain
    Is in her kiss, but wildly gay
    She laughs, and fades away,
And through the dim wood floats the strain,
All ye who love me love in vain!

THE WILLIS-DANCERS [1]

THE moonlight floods the hollow dell:—
The dell where all the city's dead
Were laid, when oft the loud plague-bell
Filled wayfarers with sudden dread :
The accursëd plague it was that swept
The young from life, and spared the old—
Who wept and lived, and lived and wept
And mourned the silent sleepers in the dell's chill fold.

The hollow dell is fill'd with light,
The frosty radiance of the moon ;
Yet gleams there are, more weirdly bright—
And what is that slow swelling tune?
It is not any wind that blows,
For not a wafted leaf doth fall ;
What is the rustling sound that grows,
As if a low wind stirred amid the poplars tall?

[1] The *Willi* or Willis-Dancers are the spirits of those who have died untimely, youths and maidens who on earth had no fulfilment of their desires. On certain nights they hold wild phantasmal revelry on earth.

Yon white, yon pale green hues that shine—
Are they but fungus-growths that beam :
What moves by yon funereal pine—
What haunts the pool where marsh-fires gleam ?
From out the shadow-haunted trees,
Along the nested hedgerows dumb,
And o'er the moonlit sloping leas
Singing a thin strange song the Willis-dancers come.

In hurrying scores, with silent feet,
In weird processional array
They pass, with motions wild and fleet :
And now they gain the common way.
Adown the long white road they flit,
Slow-singing their unechoing song,
Till, where the Calvary, moonlit,
Crowns the low hill—round whose white base the
                                        [dancers throng.

Fair, fair, unutterably fair,
With wild and gleaming eyes they pray
O for the breath of mortal air,
O for the joys grown faint and gray !
But never the carven god commands ;
The frozen eyes nor gleam nor glance—
The Willis-folk ring phantom-hands,
Then laugh and mock and whirl away in frantic
                                        [dance.

Wild, wild the dance, with blazing eyes,
With flowing hair, and faun-like leaps,
With thrilling shouts, and ecstasies.
Now one withdraws, and wails, and weeps :
Her grave-blanch'd hair around her thrown,
Her white hands claspt, she doth not hear
A voice that claims her for his own,
Nor hearkens her dead Lover call in awful fear.

For oft when from the grave they've fled
To gain phantasmal joys on earth—
Fair youths and maids who ne'er were wed
But died within their spring-time mirth—
A fearful thing hath happ'd to some :
A joyous dancer hath withdrawn,
Hath wailed and wept, and then grown dumb,
And paled, and pass'd away ev'n as the stars at
                                          [dawn.

The wan soul, with its burning gaze
From hollow eyes with anguish fill'd,
Would fain the lapsing maiden raise :
One moment all her being is thrilled
With one wild passionate desire—
Then, as a flame that is blown out,
Or as a mist in the sun's fire
She fades into the silence round the whirling rout.

Still wilder, swifter grows the fray :
Youths who on earth had lived in vain,
Maids who had yearned the livelong day
For ease to love's imperious pain;
All whose high hopes had come to nought,
All who for life's delights had striven,
All who had suffered, dreamt, or wrought
To make of our common Earth a glowing Heaven—

All, all, with eager, frantic haste
Swift dart and glide and dance and spring—
As gnats above a stagnant waste
Will interweave in a mazy ring—
With locks that once were living gold
Tossed wildly in the moonlit air,
With panting breasts that ne'er were cold
In the dear vanish'd days ere death came unaware :

Lovers who knew no joy of love
In the old barren years of life,
Together now enraptured move,
Claspt each to each with rapture rife :
Bosom to panting bosom pressed,
Hot lips athirst on thirsting lips,
Strange joys and languors doubly blest—
Snatch'd from the sombre grave, yea even from Death's
                                        [eclipse !

Swift, swifter grows the mystic dance
More wild, more wild, each fierce embrace :
The woe of death's inheritance
Gleams ghastly on each wildered face ;
A wan grey light illumes the head
Of the carv'd god to whom they prayed ;
A halt—a hush—among the dead !
A long-drawn sigh—and lo, the Willis-dancers fade !

THE COVES OF CRAIL

THE moon-white waters wash and leap,
  The dark tide floods the Coves of Crail;
Sound, sound he lies in dreamless sleep,
  Nor hears the sea-wind wail.

The pale gold of his oozy locks,
  Doth hither drift and thither wave;
His thin hands plash against the rocks,
  His white lips nothing crave.

Afar away she laughs and sings—
  A song he loved, a wild sea-strain—
Of how the mermen weave their rings
  Upon the reef-set main.

Sound, sound he lies in dreamless sleep,
  Nor hears the sea-wind wail,
Though with the tide his white hands creep
  Amid the Coves of Crail.

A DREAM

Last night thro' a haunted land I went,
Upon whose margins Ocean leant
   Waveless and soundless save for sighs
That with the twilight airs were blent.

And passing, hearing never stir
Of footfall, or the startled whirr
   Of birds, I said, " In this land lies
Sleep's home, the secret haunt of her."

And then I came upon a stone
Whereon these words were writ alone,
   The soul who reads, its body dies
Far hence that moment without moan.

And then I knew that I was dead,
And that the shadow overhead
   Was not the darkness of the skies
But that from which my soul had fled.

THE WANDERING VOICE

THEY hear it in the sunless dale,
   It moans beside the stream,
They hear it when the woodlands wail,
   And when the storm-winds scream.

They hear it,—going from the fields
   Through twilight-shadows home,—
It sighs across the silent wealds
   And far and wide doth roam.

It moans upon the wind *No more*
   The House of Torquil stands;
It comes at dusk, and o'er and o'er
   Haunts Torquil's lands.

He rides down by the foaming linn—
   But hark! what is it calls
With faint far voice, so shrill and thin,
   The House of Torquil falls.

He lifts the revel-cup at night—
   What makes him start and stare,
What makes his face blanch deadly white,
   What makes him spring from where

His comrades feast within the room,
   And through the darkness go—
What is that wailing cry of doom,
   That scream of woe!

No more in sunless dell, or high
   On moorland ways is heard the moan
Of the long-wandering prophecy:—
   In moonlit nights alone

A shadowy shape is seen to stand
   Beside a ruin'd place:
It waves a wildly threatening hand,
   It hath a dreadful face.

THE TWIN-SOUL

IN the dead of the night a spirit came:
Her moonwhite face and her eyes of flame
Were known to me:—I called her name—
    The name that shall not be spoken at all
    Till Death hath this body of mine in thrall!

And she laughed to see me lying there,
Wrapped in the living-corpse bloody and fair,
And my soul 'mid its thin films shining bare—
    And I rose and followed her glance so sweet
    And passed from the house with noiseless feet.

I know not myself what I knew, what I saw:
I know that it filled me with trouble and awe,
With pain that still at my heart doth gnaw:
    That she with her wild eyes witched my soul
    And whispered the name of the Unknown Goal.

O wild was her laugh, and wild was my cry
When with one long flash and a weary sigh
I awoke as from sleep bewilderingly:
    Her voice, her eyes, they are with me still,
    O Spirit-Enchantress, O Demon-Will!

THE ISLE OF LOST DREAMS

THERE is an Isle beyond our ken,
Haunted by Dreams of weary men.
Grey Hopes enshadow it with wings
Weary with burdens of old things:
There the insatiate water-springs
Rise with the tears of all who weep:
And deep within it, deep, oh deep
The furtive voice of Sorrow sings.
    There evermore,
    Till Time be o'er,
Sad, oh so sad, the Dreams of men
Drift through the Isle beyond our ken.

THE DEATH-CHILD

SHE sits beneath the elder-tree
And sings her song so sweet,
And dreams o'er the burn that darksomely
Runs by her moonwhite feet.

Her hair is dark as starless night,
Her flower-crown'd face is pale,
But O her eyes are lit with light
Of dread ancestral bale.

She sings an eerie song, so wild
With immemorial dule—
Though young and fair Death's mortal child
That sits by that dark pool.

And oft she cries an eldritch scream
When red with human blood
The burn becomes a crimson stream,
A wild, red, surging flood:

Or shrinks, when some swift tide of tears—
The weeping of the world—
Dark eddying 'neath man's phantom-fears
Is o'er the red stream hurl'd.

For hours beneath the elder-tree
She broods beside the stream;
Her dark eyes filled with mystery,
Her dark soul rapt in dream.

The lapsing flow she heedeth not
Through deepest depths she scans:
Life is the shade that clouds her thought,
As Death's the eclipse of man's.

·Time seems but as a bitter thing
Remember'd from of yore:
Yet ah (she thinks) her song she'll sing
When Time's long reign is o'er.

Erstwhiles she bends alow to hear
What the swift water sings,
The torrent running darkly clear
With secrets of all things.

And then she smiles a strange sad smile
And lets her harp lie long;
The death-waves oft may rise the while,
She greets them with no song.

Few ever cross that dreary moor,
Few see that flower-crown'd head;
But whoso knows that wild song's lure
Knoweth that he is dead.

OF THE SOUTH:

SOSPIRI DI ROMA

" N'être que toi, mon Rêve."

SOSPIRI DI ROMA

PRELUDE

(TO ——————————————)

"Supra un munti sparman stu bellu ciuri!
Chistu è lu ciuri di la tò billizza."

SICILIAN CANZUNO.

IN a grove of ilex
Of oak and of chestnut,
Far on the sunswept
Heights of Tusculum,
There groweth a blossom,
A snow-white bloom,
Which many have heard of,
But few have seen.
Oft bright as the morning,
Oft pale as moonlight,
There in the greenness,
In shadow and sunshine
It grows, awaiting
The hand that shall pluck it:

85

For this blossom springeth
From the heart of a poet
And of her who loved him
In the long ago,
Here on the sunswept
Heights of Tusculum.
And them it awaiteth,
Deep lovers only,
Kindred of those
Who loved and passioned
There, and whose hearts'-blood
Wrought from the Earth
This marvellous blossom
The Shadow-Lily,
The Flower of Dream.

Few that shall see it,
Fewer still
Those that shall pluck it:
But whoso gathers
That snow-white blossom
Shall love for ever,
For the passionate breath
Of the Shadow-Lily
Is Deathless Joy:
And whoso plucks it, keeps it, treasures it,
Has sunshine ever
About the heart,
Deep in the heart immortal sunshine:
For this is the gift of the snow-white blossom,
This is the gift of the Flower of Dream.

SUSURRO

BREATH o' the grass,
Ripple of wandering wind,
Murmur of tremulous leaves:
A moonbeam moving white
Like a ghost across the plain:
A shadow on the road:
And high up, high,
From the cypress-bough,
A long sweet melancholy note.
Silence.
And the topmost spray
Of the cypress-bough is still
As a wavelet in a pool:
The road lies duskily bare:
The plain is a misty gloom:
Still are·the tremulous leaves;
Scarce a last ripple of wind,
Scarce a breath i' the grass.
Hush: the tired wind sleeps:
Is it the wind's breath, or
Breath o' the grass.

HIGH NOON AT MIDSUMMER
ON THE CAMPAGNA

HIGH noon,
And from the purple-veilèd hills
To where Rome lies in azure mist,
Scarce any breath of wind
Upon this vast and solitary waste,
These leagues of sunscorch'd grass
Where i' the dawn the scrambling goats maintain
A hardy feast,
And where, when the warm yellow moonlight floods
    the flats,
Gaunt laggard sheep browse spectrally for hours,
While not less gaunt and spectral shepherds stand
Brooding, or with hollow vacant eyes
Stare down the long perspectives of the dusk.
Now not a breath:
No sound;
No living thing,
Save where the beetle jars his bristling shards,
Or where the hoarse cicala fills
The heavy heated hour with palpitant whirr.
Yet hark !
Comes not a low deep whisper from the ground,
A sigh as though the immemorial past

Breathed here a long, slow, breath?
Lost nations sleep below; an empire here
Is dust; and deeper, deeper still,
Dim shadowy peoples are the mould that warms
The roots of every flower that blooms and blows:
Even as we, too, bloom and fade,
Frail human flowers, who are so bitter fain
To be as the wind that bloweth evermore,
To be as this dread waste that shroudeth all
In garments green of grass and wilding sprays,
To be as the Night that dies not, but forever
Weaves her immortal web of starry fires;
To be as Time itself,
Time, whose vast holocausts
Lie here, deep buried from the ken of men,
Here, where no breath of wind
Ruffles the brooding heat,
The breathless blazing heat
Of Noon.

FIOR DI MEMORIA

"…. ed ogni vento
Che passa accoglie sulle tepidi ali
I sospiri d'amor di mille rose."
ENRICO NENCIONI.

FROM the swamp the white mist stealeth,
Wendeth slowly through the grasses,
Like a long lithe snake it circleth
Breathing from its mouth its poison,
Breathing fumes of the malaria.
Up the grassy slope it passeth,
Is a snake no more but changes
To a thin white veil of smoke-drift,
White as when the warm Scirocco
Blows across wet meadows gleaming
In the sudden glare of sunshine.
Thin and white upon the uplands;
Dappled, soft, as windblown swansdown,
In the sudden dips and hollows.

In the hollow where the ruins,
Immemorial ruins, columns,
Prostrate all, with strange devices,
Sculptured 'neath the yellow lichen,

In the hollow where the ruins
Lie as when the earthquake shook them
From their ancient stately beauty
Long ere Rome had gathered slowly
Round the sacred fane of Saturn,
There the grass is tall as wild-rice,
Tall as is the wind-waved bulrush
Rustling by the Tiber-marshes.
Nought is seen around but grasses,
Flower-filled grasses, lizard-haunted,
Musical with many whisperings
And the loud crescendo humming
Of the wild-bees coming, going,
And the myriad things that flitter,
Breathe, and gleam, and swift evanish
Mid these tortuous dim savannahs,
These gigantic grass-stem forests.
Nought above, but the blue hollow
With its infinite depths of azure.
Nought to meet the wandering vision
But the ruins mid the grasses,
But the windied grasses swaying
Up and billowing o'er the margins
Of the lone mist-haunted hollow,
But the wide deep dome of purple,
Cloudless, speckless, save when darkling
For a moment drifts a shadow
Far in the aerial distance,
Though no sound is borne earthward
Of the scream of that wild eagle
Whirling from his Volscian eyrie,

Where the green gloom of the grasses
Turns at noon to amber dayshine.
There the fallen ruins are covered
With a wilderness of roses:
Roses, roses, in such masses
That the fangless snakes which wander
Deep within their pliant coverts
Sink and rise and glide and vanish
As though swimming in sweet waters
Where each wavelet curdles rosily
To a blossoming bud, or floateth
Calmly as a smooth soft roseleaf.
Oh, the wilderness of roses
Shrouding all the fallen columns,
All the mossy lichen'd marbles:
Fragrant depths of crimson roses,
Carmine, pink, some wanly yellow
As young lime-leaves in the dawnlight,
Some as ivory of India
Deftly wrought by patient fingers
In the dim mysterious ages;
Others wan as surf in starlight,
Dusky white as coral garnered
In the deeps where light a dream is,
Ruffling the swart glooms of Ocean:
But damask most, or crimson, blood-red,
Flushed as wine-stained, or as dawn-clouds.
Mass on mass of tangled roses,
Blossom-flames, or multitudinous
Plumes of those lost birds of Eden
Which, as in long roseate vapours,

With a myriad wings waft upward
Each new morn, and with the sunrise
Earthward sweep on glowing pinions,
Till they wheel and fade and vanish
On their endless quest of Eden.
One vast crimson flood of roses,
Whence a carven stone or column
Reareth sometimes as a boulder
Swart upborne o'er sunset-waters.
Oh the fragrance when the south-wind,
When the languorous Scirocco
Breathes with tepid breath upon them,
And with idle feet strays lightly
O'er and o'er their billowy sweetness.
Nought but this flushed sea of roses,
And the green gloom of the grasses
Shrouding the forgotten ruins
In the lone mist-haunted hollow,
Lost, unseen, but domed in splendour
By the depths of purple azure.

Lo, amidst the roses' tangle
What white sunlit beauty shineth?
Some stone goddess, nymph, or naiad,
Carven in the bygone ages,
Wan as ivory now, and glowing
With the multitudinous breaths of sunlight?
Nay, no marble this that gleameth
Ivory-white among the roses,
For the naked flesh moves gently
With the breath that rising, falling,

Scarcely stirs the fluttered roseleaves.
O wild mountain-girl, whom never
Lover yet has won with passion,
But whose arms have claspt the hill-wind,
But whose swelling breast has quivered
'Neath the soft south-wind's caresses,
Whose white limbs have felt the kisses
Of the wandering wind, thy lover:
O wild mountain-girl, sleep ever,
Naked there in all thy beauty
Mid the sea of clustering roses,
Lost within the green-glooms tender
Of the wind-swayed desert-grasses.
Dark thy cloud of hair about thee,
Dark thy shadowy eyes that dream
Far into the azure distance:
White thy limbs as sunlit ivory,
With stray roseleaves scattered o'er them,
With thy sea of roses round thee.
What strange dreams are thine, O Goddess—
Goddess, surely, for beyond thee
Sways a cloud of fluttering sparrows:
Ah, is it thou — nay, never goddess
Now to mortal man discloseth
That serene immortal beauty,
Which is as a draught of rapture
Fraught with bitterness and sorrow:
I have tasted, quaffed it, Goddess,
For the soul can know and see thee,
For the soul can woo and win thee,
Thee, even thee, O Beautiful !

I have drunk its perilous rapture,
Knowing all have quaffed and feared not,
And have known the bitter savour:
Yet, would drink again, O Goddess !

Nay, no goddess here, but only,
Naked, dreaming in the sunshine,
Ivory-white among the roseleaves,
With her dark hair thrown about her
Like the dusk about the morning,
Only a wild mountain-girl,
Filled with secret springs of passion,
Immemorial seeds of passion
Wrought at last through generations
In this perfect flower of beauty
To a strange unspeakable longing.
In a blaze of heat the sunlight,
Fierce with torrid fires of Junetide,
Beats upon her white limbs gleaming
In the sunlit flames of roses:
But she moves not, though a quiver
Ofttimes passes like a tremor
Shimmering through the furthest eastward
Ere the stars grow suddenly paler.

O wild mountain-girl, sleep ever,
Naked there in all thy beauty
Mid the sea of clustering roses:
Deep within thy sea of roses
Sink to slumber, sweeter, deeper,
Where no waking is, but dreams are

Changed to roses that shall hide thee,
That shall hide thee and enshroud thee
There within thy grassy hollow:
Where the winds alone shall call thee,
And the marish-mist shall wander
Like a ghost between the grasses,
In among the buried columns
Lost within thy ruin of roses.

THE FOUNTAIN OF THE ACQUA PAOLA

NOT where thy turbid wave
Flowing Maremma-ward,
Moves heavily, Tiber,
Through Rome the Eternal,
Not there her music, not there her joy is:
But rather where the tall pines
On the Janiculum heights
Sing their high song, with deeper therein, like an echo
Heard in a mountain-hollow where cataracts break,
A sound as of surge and of foaming:
Yes, there where the echoing pines
Whisper to high wandering winds
The rush and the surge and the splendour
Where the Acqua Paola thunders
Into its fount gigantic,
With noise like a tempest cleaving
With mighty wings
The norland forests.

From dayspring, yellow and green
And grey as a swan's breastfeather,
To sunset's amber and gold
And the white star of dusk,

And through the moonwhite hours
Till only Hesperus hangs
His quivering tremulous disc
O'er the faint-flushed forehead of Dawn—
All hours, all days, forever
Surgeth the singing flood,
With chant and paean glorious,
With foam and splash and splendour,
A music wild, barbaric,
That calleth loud over Rome,
Laughing, mocking, rejoicing:
The sound of the waves when Ocean
Laughs at the vanishing land
And, fronting her shoreless leagues,
Remembers the ruined empires
That now are the drift and shingle
In cavernous hollows under
Her zone of Oblivion,
Silence that nought shall break,
Eternal calm.

Foam, spray and splendour
Of rushing waters,
Grey-blue as the pale blue dome
That circleth the morning star
While still his fires are brighter
Than the wanwhite fire of the moon.
Foam, spray, and surge
Of rushing waters !
O the hot flood of sunshine
Yellowly pouring

Over and into thee, jubilant Fountain:
Thy cataracts filled
With vanishing rainbows,
Shimmering lights
As though the Aurora's
Wild polar fires
Flashed in thy happy bubbles, died in thy foam.

Ever in joyous laughter
Thy wavelets are dancing,
Little waves with crests bright with sunlight
Tossing their foamy arms,
Laughing and leaping,
Whirling, inweaving,
Rippling at last and sleepily laving
The mossed stone-barriers
That clasp them round.
Bright too and joyous,
They, in the moonshine,
When the falling waters
Are as wreaths of snow
Falling for ever
Down mountain-flanks,
Like melting snows
In the high hill-hollows
Seen from the valleys
And seeming to fall,
To fall forever
A flower of water,
Silent, and stirred not
By any wind.

Bright too and joyous
In darkling nights,
When the moon shroudeth
Her face in a veil
Of cloudy vapours,
Or, like a flower
I' the wane of its beauty,
Droopeth and falleth
Till lost to sight,
Stoopeth and fadeth
Into the dark—
Or when like a sickle
Thin and silvern
She moveth slowly
Through the starry fields,
Moveth slowly
Mid the flowers of the stars
In the harvest-fields
Of Eternity:
Bright too and joyous,
For then the shadows
Play with the foam-lights,
With the flying whiteness,
And snowy surging.
But brighter, more joyous,
Save when the moon-flower
In all her splendour
Floats on thy bosom,
Or, rather, dreameth
Deep in the heart of thee
O happy Fountain:

Brighter, more joyous,
Then, when amidst thee,
Strewn through thy waters,
The stars are sown
As seed multitudinous,
As silvern seed
In thy shadowy-furrows:
Seed of the skiey flowers
That in the heavens
Bloom forever,
Blossoms and blooms of
Eternal splendour.
Then is thy joy most,
O jubilant Fountain,
Then are thy waters
Sweetest of song,
Then do thy waters
Surge, leap, rejoicing,
Lave, and lapse slowly
To haunted stillness
And darkling dreams:
Then is thy music rarest,
Wildest and sweetest
Music of Rome—
Rome the Eternal,
Through whose heart of shadow
Moveth slowly
Flowing Maremma-ward
Thy murmur, Tiber,
Thy muffled voice,
Whom none interpreteth

But boding, ominous,
Is as the sound of
Murmurous seas
Heard afar inland—
There, where Maremma-ward
Flowing heavily,
Moveth, Tiber,
Thy sullen wave.

PRIMO SOSPIRO DI PRIMAVERA

*(Noon: First of February: On the Corsini Terraces
on the Janiculum)*

BOOM!
The gun has thundered forth the hour of Noon!
High upon the wings of Tramontana
Swells a storm of bells,
From a thousand churches, convents, buildings,
Clanging, jangling, intermingling,
Softened to a joyous music
Borne upward by the wind
To the heights already sounding
With the surge of the three fountains
Of the Acqua Paola torrent,
To the heights already echoing
With the Tramontana's challenge
Tossed with reckless glee and laughter
Through the ilexes and stone-pines.
What a sound as of the ocean
When the tides are driving inland,
And the rampant waves are leaping

Swift before the scourging sea-wind!
And through all the windy tumult
How the bells go wildly echoing,
Like a storm of voices calling
Far o'er mist-beleaguered waters.
Suddenly silence: even the wind swings
For a brief space skyward, chasing
The last flying ragged cloudlets:
Then from out the ilex-avenue
Rings with palpitant, thrilling rapture,
Clear and sweet, the first spring-music
Of the speckle-breasted storm-thrush!
Swish-sh-sh! the wind again, the medley
Of its strong wings beating wildly,
Spray-wet, filled with piny odours.

Silence where the herald-thrush first
Took the break of Spring with rapture.
Yet what song in all the springtide
Shall be sweeter, rarer, wilder,
Than the sudden burst of music,
Sung from utter joy and wonder
Ere the earliest limes have budded:
Than that momentary outburst
When the bells of noon had fallen
To an ebbing tide of music
Down the sounding shores of Roma,
And the turbulent Tramontana
Had far skyward swept, with pinions
Hawk-like spread to swoop upon the

Flying drifts of ragged cloudlets !
O the bells of Rome, the clamour
Of the joyous Tramontana,
O the wildness of thy music,
Rapturous thrush, last Spring remembering,
With thy lost voice freed one moment
From its long forlorn silence !
Spring is here—and Rome—together !

CLOUDS

(Agro   Romano)

As though the dead cities
Of the ancient time
Were builded again
In the heights of heaven,
With spires of amber
And golden domes,
Wide streets of topaz and amethyst ways;
Far o'er the pale blue waste,
Oft purple-shadowed,
Of the Agro Romano,
Rises the splendid
City of Cloud.
There must the winds be soft as the twilight
Invisibly falling when the daystar has wester'd;
There must the rainbows trail up through the sunlight.
So fair are the hues on those white snowy masses.
Mountainous glories,
They move superbly;
Crumbling so slowly,
That none perceives when
The golden domes
Are sunk in the valleys

Of fathomless snow,
Or when, in silence,
The loftiest spires
Fade into smoke, or as vapour that passeth
When the hot breath of noon
Thirsts through the firmament.
Beautiful, beautiful,
The City of Cloud,
In splendour ruinous,
With golden domes,
And spires of amber,
Builded superbly
In the heights of heaven.

A DREAM AT ARDEA

(*Maremma*)

WHERE Ardea, the cliff-girt,
Looks to the Sea,
Dreaming forever
In her desert place
Of her vanished glory—
There too in the tall grass,
Starred with narcissus
And the flaming poppy,
I dreamed a dream.

Not of the days when
The fierce trumpeting
Of the Asian elephants
Made the wild horses
Snort in new terror,
Snort and wheel wildly,
Till o'er the Campagna
They passed like a trail
Of vanishing smoke.
No, nor when
The brazen clarions
Of the Roman legion
Summoned the hill-folk

To the Punic War:
Nor yet when the shadow
Of the falling star
Of the house of Tarquin
Swept unseen o'er the banquet,
And none, foreseeing,
Drew forth the pure sword
For the foul heart of Sextus.
Nor yet of the ancient days
When the fierce Rutuli
Laughed at the boasting of
The seven-hilled city,
And when on rude altars
White victims lay,
To appease the anger
Of barbarian Gods—
Nay, not of these, not even the far-off,
The ancient time, when the mother of Perseus,
Danaë the beautiful, came hither and builded
Close to the sea the hill-town which standeth
Now amid leagues of the inland grasses,
White with the surf of the blossoming asphodels—
Nay, but only
Of the shrine of her,
Venus, the Beautiful One,
The Well-Beloved.
Lost, it lieth
Deep mid the tangle,
Deep 'neath the roots of the flowers and the grasses
Drawn like a veil o'er
The face of Maremma.

Only the brown lark
Singing above it,
Only the hare
Beneath the wild olive,
Only the linnet aflit in the myrtle,
Only the spotted snake
Writhing swiftly
O'er the thyme and the spikenard,
Only the falcon
Dusking a moment the gold of the yellow broom,
Only the things of the air and the desert,
Know where deep in the maze of the undergrowth
Lieth the shrine of the sacred Goddess,
The shrine of Venus.
Up through the dark blue mist of the harebells—
All the wild glory, with trailing convolvulus,
Lenten lilies asway in the sunlight,
Wine-dark anemones, pasque-flowers of ruby,
Iris and daffodil and sweet smelling violet,
And high over all the white and gold shining
Where the wind raced o'er the asphodel meadows:
All the flower-glory of Spring in Maremma,
But here, just here, a mist of the harebells—
Up through the dark blue mist of the harebells
Rose like a white smoke hovering gently
Over the windless woodlands of Ostia
Where the charcoal-burners wander like shadows,
Rose a white vapour, stealthily, slowly.

Ah, but the wonder ! the wan ghost of Venus
Rose slowly before me:

Dark, deep, and awful the eyes of the vision,
Sad beyond words that wraith of dead beauty,
Chill now and solemn,
Austere as the grave,
The face that had blanched
The high gods of old,
The face that had led
The heroes of men
From the heights of Caucasus
To the uttermost ends
Of Earth, as leadeth nightly
The Moon, her cohorts
Of perishing billows.
" I am she whom thou lovest ":
" *Nay, whom I worship, Goddess and Queen!* "
" I am she whom thou worshippest " :
" *For thou art Beauty, and Beauty I worship,*
" *And thou art Love, and Love—*
" Love is Beauty.   They love not nor worship,
" They who dissever the one from the other ":
" *Hearken, O Goddess !* "
" Nay, shadow of shadows, why callest me Goddess !
Far from thy world "the Goddess" is banished.
Ye have chosen the dark: the dark be with you !
Ye have chosen sorrow: and sorrow is yours:
O fools that worship vain Gods, and know not
That life is the breath but of perishing dust—
They only live in whose hearts there hath fallen
The breath of my passion—
" *O Goddess, fade not !* "
" I pass, and behold,

With my passing goeth
The joy of the world."

Darkly austere
The face of the Goddess.
Then like a flame
That groweth wan
And flickereth forth from the reach of vision,
The face of Venus
Was seen no more,
Though through the mist
Her eyes gleamed darkly,
Great fires of joy—
Of joy disherited,
But glorious ever
In their lordly scorn,
Their high disdain.

Not till the purple-hued
Wings of the twilight
Waved softly downward
From the Alban hills,
And moved stilly
Over the vast dim leagues of Maremma,
Turned I backward
My wandering steps.
Far o'er the white-glimmering
Breast of the Tyrrhene Sea
(Laid as in sleep at the feet of the hills)
Rose, dropping liquid fires
Into the wine-dark vault of the heaven,

The Star of Evening,
Venus, the Evening Star:
Eternal, serene,
In deathless beauty
Revolving ever
Through the stellar spheres !

High o'er the shadowy heights
Of the Volscian summits
The full moon soared:
Soared slowly upward
Like a golden nenuphar
In a vaster Nilus
Than that which floweth
Through the heart of Egypt.
The moon that maketh
The world so beautiful,
That moveth so tenderly
Over desolate things,
The moon that giveth
The amber light,
Wherein best blossom
The mystic flowers
Of human love.

Through the darkness
Whelming the waste,
And, like a stealthy tide
Rising around
Ardea, the cliff-girt,
Wavered the sound of joyous laughter.

Sweet words and sweeter
Fell where the lentisc
Bloomed, and the rosemary:
Loving caresses
Lost in a rustle
Where the hawthorn-bushes
Loomed large in the twilight
Of the fireflies' lanterns.

Deep in the heart of
A myrtle-thicket
A nightingale stirred:
With low sweet note,
Thrilling strangely,
And as though moving
With the breath of her passion
The midmost leaves.
But once her plaint :—
Then wild and glad,
In a free ecstasy,
In utter bliss,
In one high whirl of rapture, sang
His answering song
Her mate, low swaying upon a bough,
With throat full-strained, and quivering wings
Beating with tremulous whirr.

Then I was glad,
For surely I knew
I had dreamed a dream 'neath the spell of Maremma.
Not sunk in the drift

Of antique dust,
Lost from the ken of Earth
Within her shrine,
Venus, the Beautiful,
The Queen of Love !
But though no longer
Beheld of man,
Still living and breathing
Through the heart of the world—
Whether in the song,
Passionate, beautiful,
Of the nightingale;
Or in the glad rapture
Of lovers meeting,
With soft caresses
Hid in the dusk;
In the fair flower of the vast field of heaven;
Or in the glow,
The pulsing splendour,
Of the white star of joy,
The Star of Eve.

RED POPPIES

(In the Sabine valleys near Rome)

THROUGH the seeding grass,
And the tall corn,
The wind goes:
With nimble feet,
And blithe voice,
Calling, calling,
The wind goes
Through the seeding grass,
And the tall corn.

What calleth the wind,
Passing by—
The shepherd-wind?
Far and near
He laugheth low,
And the red poppies
Lift their heads
And toss i' the sun.
A thousand thousand blooms
Tost i' the air,

Banners of joy,
For 'tis the shepherd-wind
Passing by,
Singing and laughing low
Through the seeding grass
And the tall corn.

.

THE WHITE PEACOCK

HERE where the sunlight
Floodeth the garden,
Where the pomegranate
Reareth its glory
Of gorgeous blossom;
Where the oleanders
Dream through the noontides;
And, like surf o' the sea
Round cliffs of basalt,
The thick magnolias
In billowy masses
Front the sombre green of the ilexes:
Here where the heat lies
Pale blue in the hollows,
Where blue are the shadows
On the fronds of the cactus,
Where pale blue the gleaming
Of fir and cypress,
With the cones upon them
Amber or glowing
With virgin gold:
Here where the honey-flower
Makes the heat fragrant,
As though from the gardens
Of Gulistân,

Where the bulbul singeth
Through a mist of roses,
A breath were borne:
Here where the dream-flowers,
The cream-white poppies
Silently waver,
And where the Scirocco,
Faint in the hollows,
Foldeth his soft white wings in the sunlight,
And lieth sleeping
Deep in the heart of
A sea of white violets:
Here, as the breath, as the soul of this beauty
Moveth in silence, and dreamlike, and slowly,
White as a snow-drift in mountain-valleys
When softly upon it the gold light lingers:
White as the foam o' the sea that is driven
O'er billows of azure agleam with sun-yellow:
Cream-white and soft as the breasts of a girl,
Moves the White Peacock, as though through the
                                         [noontide
A dream of the moonlight were real for a moment.
Dim on the beautiful fan that he spreadeth,
Foldeth and spreadeth abroad in the sunlight,
Dim on the cream-white are blue adumbrations,
Shadows so pale in their delicate blueness
That visions they seem as of vanishing violets,
The fragrant white violets veinëd with azure,
Pale, pale as the breath of blue smoke in far woodlands.
Here, as the breath, as the soul of this beauty,
White as a cloud through the heats of the noontide
Moves the White Peacock.

THE SWIMMER OF NEMI

(The Lake of Nemi: September)

WHITE through the azure,
The purple blueness,
Of Nemi's waters
The swimmer goeth.
Ivory-white, or wan white as roses
Yellowed and tanned by the suns of the Orient,
His strong limbs sever the violet hollows;
A shimmer of white fantastic motions
Wavering deep through the lake as he swimmeth.
Like gorse in the sunlight the gold of his yellow hair,
Yellow with sunshine and bright as with dew-drops,
Spray of the waters flung back as he tosseth
His head i' the sunlight in the midst of his laughter:
Red o'er his body, blossom-white mid the blueness,
And trailing behind him in glory of scarlet,
A branch of the red-berried ash of the mountains.
White as a moon-beam
Drifting athwart
The purple twilight,
The swimmer goeth —
Joyously laughing,
With o'er his shoulders,

Agleam in the sunshine
The trailing branch
With the scarlet berries.
Green are the leaves, and scarlet the berries,
White are the limbs of the swimmer beyond them,
Blue the deep heart of the still, brooding lakelet,
Pale-blue the hills in the haze of September,
The high Alban hills in their silence and beauty,
Purple the depths of the windless heaven
Curv'd like a flower o'er the waters of Nemi.

AL FAR DELLA NOTTE

HARK!
As a bubbling fount
That suddenly wells
And rises in tall spiral waves and flying spray,
The high, sweet, quavering, throbbing voice
Of the nightingale!
Not yet the purple veil of dusk has fallen,
But o'er the yellow band
That binds the west
The vesper star beats like the pulse of heaven.

Up from the fields
The peasants troop,
Singing their songs of love:
And oft the twang of thin string'd music breaks
High o'er the welcoming shouts,
The homing laughter.
The whirling bats are out,
And to and fro
The blue swifts wheel
Where, i' the shallows of the dusk,
The grey moths flutter
Over the pale blooms
Of the night-flowering bay.

Softly adown the slopes,
And o'er the plain,
Ave Maria
Solemnly soundeth.
The long day is over.
Dusk, and silence now:
And Night, that is as dew
On the Flower of the World.

THISTLEDOWN

(Spring on the Campagna)

BLOWETH like snow
From the grey thistles
The thistledown:
And the fairy-feathers
O' the dandelion
Are tossed by the breeze
Hither and thither:
Over the grasses,
The seeding grasses
Where the poppies shake
And the campions waver,
And where the clover,
Purple and white,
Fills leagues with the fragrance
Of sunsweet honey;
Hither and thither
The fairy-feathers
O' the dandelion,
And white puff-balls
O' the thistledown,
Merrily dancing,
Light on the breeze,

Wheeling and sailing,
And laughing to scorn
The butterflies
And the moths of azure;
Blowing like snow
Or foam o' the sea,
Hither and thither
Upward and downward.

Now for a moment
A thistledown
On a white ball resteth,
Sunbleached and hollow;
A human skull
Of the ancient days,
When Sabines and Latins
Made all the land here
As red with blood
As it now is scarlet
With flaming poppies.
Now the feathers
O' the dandelion,
Like sunlit swansdown
Long tost by the wind
O'er the laughter of waters,
Are blown like surf
On a hidden rock —
A broken arch
Of a Roman temple,
Where long, long ago,
The swarthy priests

Worshipped their Gods,
The Gods now less than
The very dust
Whence the green grass springeth.
But for a moment, then the wind takes them,
Blows them, plays with them,
Tosses them high through the gold of the sunshine,
Wavers them upward, wavers them downward,
Hither and thither among the white butterflies,
Over and under the blue-moths and honey-bees,
Over the leagues of blossoming clover,
Purple and white, the sweet-smelling clover,
Far o'er the grasses,
And grey hanging thistles,
Hither and thither
Are floating and sailing
The fairy-feathers
O' the dandelion,
Bloweth like snow
The joy o' the meadows,
The thistledown.

THE TWO RUINS

A SEA of moonlight.
And in the sea an isle
Black, rugged, tempest-torn, vast :
O mighty Colosseum
More grand in this thy ruin
Than when proud Cæsar smiled, and all thy walls
Rang with tumultuous acclaim,
While round thy dark foundations moaned
A wind of alien pain.
Terrible thou, O splendour of the Past.
How great the Rome that knew thee, and how dread!
Proud Roman, thine inheritance
Is as a deathless crown,
Yea, as a crown deep-set upon the brows,
The unfurrowed front of Time that is to be.

Hark, that low whine !
What crippled thing is this,
This spume of vice,
This wreck of high estate ?
What ruin this that rises gaunt and wild :
Thou, thou art Rome, the Past,
The Rome that is !

Not here a venerable age,
But dull decay,
Slow death, and utter weariness.
Yon vast forlorn walls are but the frozen surf
Of tides long ages ebbed :
In thee Ruin is, in thee and such as thee.

THE SHEPHERD

(Near the Theatre of Marcellus : Piazza Montanara)

SOLITARY he stands,
Clad in his goat-skins,
Though all about him
The busy throng
Cometh and goeth.
Overhead, the vast ruin,
Wind-worn, time-wrought,
Gloomily rises.
Scarce doth he note it,
Yet doth it give him
The touch of nearness,
Which the soul craves for
In alien places :
As.the strayed mariner,
Yearning, far inland,
For sight of the sea,
Smiles when he fingers a rope, or
Heareth the wind
Surge round the hedgerows
As erst through the cordage ;
Or, on the endless, dusty, white high-road,

Puts his ear to the pole
Vibrating with song, as the mast
Erewhile rang with the hum
Of the hurricane.

What doth he here,
Away from the pastures
On the desolate Campagna?
From his haggard face
Sorrowfully his wild black eyes
Stare on the weariness,
The noise, and hurry,
And surge of the traffic.
Sometimes, a faint smile
Flitteth athwart his face,
When a woman, from the well,
Passeth by with a conca
Poised on her head :
Thus oft hath he seen
The peasant girls
In the little hamlets
Far out on the plain :
Or when a wine-cart
With its tall cappoto
A-swing like a high tent windswayed sidewise,
Rattles in from the Appian highway,
White with the dust of the Alban hills.
What doth he here,
He in whose eyes are
The passion of the desert :
He in whose ears rings

The free music
Of the winds that wander
Through the desert-ruins?
Not here, O Shepherd.
Would'st thou fain dwell,
Though in the Holy City
God's Regent lives :
Better the desolate waste,
Better the free lone life,
For there thou canst breathe,
There silence abideth,
There, not the Regent,
But God himself
Dwelleth and speaketh.

ALL' ORA DELLA STELLA

(*Bells of Evening*)

RING the bells of evening, through the gathering dusk;
Ring the bells upon the plain ;
Rings the bell from out the tower against the light,
Black against the west aflame, against
The sea of deepening orange, purple, yellow
(O the pale green cowslip-yellow where the crows
Fly swiftly from the dim Campagna homeward);
Ring the bells from out the little chapel yonder,
In the tiny hill-town nestling on its craggy steep.

From this lonely height where, half forgotten,
Life still lingers in unvarying round,
Can they ring away the evil sloth that broodeth
As a bat gigantic broodeth over
The low-breathing bust wherefrom it draws the life-
                          [blood ?
Can they ring away the dark and stagnant vapours
That abide with men, here, on this height—
On this height now flaming in the sunset
Like a vast carbuncle on a burning desert ?
Ring, O ring, O bells, ring, ring,

Not for peace, or rest that sweet is,
Not for happy glooms and tender,
But for storm and tempest rather,
For a fierce and surging tempest
That shall wake the mountain-hollows
With the cry of Life arising !

Rings the solitary bell upon the tower,
Where the fever-stricken monks
Kneel and pray :
Where the monks within the black and lonely tower
Dream that heaven lies yonder,
Where through seas of wondrous living yellow
The star of eve swims forth in silvern fire :
Ah, the heaven that dwelleth yonder !
Ring, O solitary bell, thy vesper,
Toll thy hymn of hopes that are as vapours,
Vapours lit a moment with strange glory
Ere they fade into the darkness following after !

Ring the bells upon the plain,
All along the misty, vague Campagna :
Unseen hamlets in the hollows, lonely dwellings
Where gaunt hermits kneel and mutter,
Scattered villages, and ruined places
Where the shepherd only sleeps and hears nought ever
Save the wild wind sweeping o'er the grasses,
Or the soft Scirocco gliding stilly
O'er the fallen columns, broken arches,
Whereamong his sheep go wandering vaguely,
Hears but these, or cry of hawk or raven,

Nightjar swooping through the moonless dusk—
Hears nought else, save in the lonely distance
The fierce sheepdogs snarling as they watch and prowl.
Softly, slow, the vesper bells are ringing
For all desolate haunts upon the waste,
For all dreary lives upon the lone Campagna,
Lives now spent like spume from ebbing waters,
Spume thrown waste to swelter in the sun,
Spume cast up and left by ebbing waters.

Ring the bells of evening through the gathering dusk :
Ring the bells upon the plain,
From the tower looming black against the light,
From the hill-town all aflame upon its steep,
Ring the bells :
Clamorous voices they, loud prayers crying
That of the perishing flames of sunset burning,
Of these red and yellow flames swift-fading yonder,
God will make new fires of sunrise splendid,
God will recreate a glorious morning.

THE MANDOLIN

Tinkle-trink, tinkle-trink, trinkle-trinkle, trink !
Hark, the mandolin !
Through the dusk the merry music falleth sweet.
Where the fountain falls,
Where the fountain falls all shimmering in the moon-
[shine white,
Tinkle-trink, tinkle-trink, trinkle-trinkle, trink!
Where the wind-stirred olives quiver,
Quiver, quiver, leaves a-quiver,
White as silver in the moonlight but like bat-wings in
[the dusk,
Where the great grey moths sail slowly
Slowly, slowly, like faint dreams
In the wildering woods of Sleep,
Where no night or day is,
But only, in dim twilights, the wan sheen
Of the Moon of Sleep.

Hark, the mandolin !
Where the dark-coned cypress rises,
Thin, more thin, till threadlike, wavering
The last spray soars up as smoke,
As a vanishing breath of incense,
To the silent stars that glimmer

In the veil of purple darkness,
The deep vault of heaven that seemeth
As a veil that falleth,
A dark veil that foldeth gently
The tired day-worn world, breathing stilly as a sleep-
[ing child.

Hark, the mandolin:
And a soft low sound of laughter !
Tinkle-trink, tinkle-trink, trinkle-trinkle, trink !

Hush: from out the cypress standing
Black against the yellow moonlight
What a thrill, what a sob, what a sudden rapture flung
Athwart the dark !
Passion of song !
Silence again, save mid the whispering leaves
The unquiet wind, that as the tide
Cometh and goeth.
Now one long thrilling note, prolonged and sweet,
And then a low swift stir,
A whirr of fluttering wings,
And, in the laurels near, two nested nightingales !
Loud, loud, the mandolin,
Tinkle-trink, tinkle-trink, trinkle-trinkle, trink,
Trink, trink, trinkle-trink !
Through the fragrant silent night it draweth near,
Ah, the low cry, the little laugh, the rustle:
Tinkle - trink — hush, a kiss — *tinkle-trink* — hush—
[hush—
Tinkle-trink, tinkle-trink, trinkle-trinkle, trink !
Where the shadows massed together

Make a hollow darkness, girt
By the yellow flood of moonshine floating by,
Where the groves of ilex whisper
In the silence, fragrant, sweet,
Where the ilexes are dreaming
In their depths of darkest shadow,
Move the fireflies slowly,
Mazily inweaving,
Interweaving, interflowing;
Wandering fires, like little lanterns
Borne by souls of birds and flowers
Seeking ever resurrection
In the gladsome world of sunshine;
Seeking vainly through the darkness
In beneath the ilex-branches
Where the very moonshine faileth,
And the dark grey moths wave wanly
Flitting from the outer gloaming.
Oh, the fragrance, and the mystery, and the silence !
Where the fireflies, mid the ilex,
Rise and fall, recross, inweave
In an endless wavy motion,
In a slow aerial dancing
In a maze of little flames
In and out the ilex-branches:
Hush ! the mandolin !
Louder still, and louder, louder:
Ah, the happy laugh, and rustle,
Rustle, rustle,
Ah the kiss, the cry, the rapture.
Silence, where the ilex-branches

Loom out faintly from their darkness
Where, slow-wandering flames, the fireflies
Rise and fall, recross, inweave
In an endless wavy motion,
In a slow aerial dancing.

Silence: not a breath is stirring:
Not a leaflet quivers faintly.
Silence: even the bats are silent
Wheeling swiftly through the upper air,
Where the gnat's thin shrilling music
Fades into the flooding moonlight:
Hush, low whispered words and kisses,
Hush, a cry of pain, of rapture.
Not a sound, a sound thereafter,
But a low sweet sigh of breathing,
And, from out the flowering laurel,
Just a twittering breath of music,
Just a long-drawn pulsing note
Of a sweet and passionate answer.
Silence: hark, a stir — low laughter —
Whispered words — and rustle — rustle —
Trink — trink — the mandolin !
Hark, it trinkles down the valley,
Trink-trink, trinkle-trink, trinkle-trink !
Past the cistus, blooming whitely,
Past the oleander-bushes,
Past the ilexes and olives,
Where the two tall pines are whispering
With the sleepy wind that foldeth

His tired pinions ere he sleepeth
On the flood of amber moonlight.
Wind o' the night, tired wind o' night —
Tinkle-trink, trink, trinkle-trink,
Trink, trinkle-trink,
Trink!

BAT-WINGS

FLITTER, flitter, through the twilight,
Pipistrello:
Where the moonshine glitters
Waver thy swart wings,
Darting hither, thither,
Swift as wheeling swallow.
Where the shadows gather
In and out thou flittest,
Flitter, flitter,
Waver, waver,
Pipistrello.
Thin thy faint aerial song is,
Thin and fainter than the shrilling
Of the gnats thou chasest wildly,
But how delicately dainty —
Thin and faint and wavering also,
In the high sweet upper air,
Where the gnats weave endless mazes
In their pyramidal dances —
And thy dusky wings go flutter,
Flutter, flutter,
Waver, waver,
But without a sound or rustle
Through the purple air of twilight.
Flitter, flitter, flutter, flitter,
Pipistrello.

LA VELIA

(The Sea-Gull: Pontine Marshes)

HERE where the marsh
Waves white with ranunculus,
Where the yellow daffodil
Flieth his banner
In the fetid air,
And oft mid the bulrushes
Rustleth the porcupine
Or surgeth the boar—
Though bloweth rarely
The fresh wind,
The Tramontana,
And only Scirocco
Heavily lifts
The feathery plumes the tall canes carry:
What dost thou here,
O bird of the ocean?
Here, where the marshes
Are never stirred
By the pulse of the tides;
Here where the white mists
Crawl on the swamp,

But never the rush and the surge of the billows?
White as a snowflake thou gleamest, and passest:
Drearier now the chill waste of the Stagno,
Wearier now the dull silence and boding.
Would that again
Thy glad presence were gleaming
Here where the marsh
Steams white in the sunshine;
For swift on my sight,
As thy white wings wavered,
Broke the sea in its beauty,
With foam, and splendour
Of rolling waves:
And loud on my ears (O the longing, the yearning)
When thy cry filled the silence,
Came the surge of the sea
And the tumult of waters.

SPUMA DAL MARE

(On the Latin Coast)

FLOWER o' the wave,
White foam of the waters,
The many-coloured:
Here blue as a harebell,
Here pale as the turquoise;
Here green as the grasses
Of mountain hollows,
Here lucent as jade when wet in the sunshine,
Here paler than apples ere ruddied by autumn.
Depths o' the purple!
Amethyst yonder,
Yonder as ling on the hills of October
With shadows as deep,
Where islets of sea-wrack
Wave in the shallows,
As the sheen of the feathers
On the blue-green breast
Of the bird of the Orient,
The splendid peacock.
Foam o' the waves,
White crests ashine
With a dazzle of sunlight!

Here the low breakers are rolling through shallows,
Yellow and muddied, the hue of the topaz
Ere cut from the boulder;
Save when the sunlight swims through them slantwise,
When inward they roll
Long billows of amber,
Crowned with pale yellow
And grey-green spume.
Here wan grey their slopes
Where the broken lights reach them,
Dull grey of pearl, and dappled, and darkling,
As when mid the high
Northward drift of the clouds,
Scirocco bloweth
With soft fanning breath.

Foam o' the waves,
Blown blossoms of ocean,
White flowers of the waters,
The many-coloured.

A WINTER EVENING

(An Hour after Nightfall, on Saturday, January 17, 1891)

[To E. W. R.]

THE wild wind in the pines
Surgeth and moaneth,
And the flying snow
Whirls hither and thither,
Tost from the sprays of the firs on the Pincio.
Here, in the dim gloomy Via dell' Mura,
Dark as a torrent in mountainous chasms,
Not a breath of the tempest waves downward upon us:
Straight down the vast mighty walls hang in silence
Ice-spears and ice-shafts, rigid, unyielding:
Here all the snow-drift lies thick and untrodden,
Cold, white, and desolate save where the red light
Gleams from a window in yonder high turret.
Loud mid the trees of the Medici gardens,
Surgeth the wind, and over the Pincio
Sweeps to the southward the drift of the snowstorm:
Clear to the northward the wan wintry moonshine
Showeth the last pines silent and moveless,
Untouched by the wild sweeping wing of the tempest.

Swift in the skies o'er the heights of the Vatican
Flash upon flash, long pulsations of lightning,
And borne afar from the distant Campagna
The long low muttering growls of the thunder.
Wild night of the tempest, with lightning and moon-
                                              [shine,
Thunder afar and the surge of the snow-blast,
The whisper of pines and the glimmer of starlight,
The voice of the wind in the woods of Borghese,
These, these together, and here in the darkness
Here in the dim, gloomy Via dell' Mura,
Nought but the peace of the snow-drift unruffled,
Whitely obscure, save where from the window
High in the walls of the Medici gardens
Glows a red shining, fierily bloodred.
What lies in the heart of thee, Night, thus so ominous?
What is thy secret, strange joy or strange sorrow?

THE BATHER

WHERE the sea-wind ruffles
The pale pink blooms
Of the fragrant Daphne,
And passeth softly
Over the sward
Of the cyclamen-blossoms,
The Bather stands.
Rosy white, as a cloud at the dawning,
Silent she stands,
And looks far seaward,
As a seabird, dreaming
On some lone rock,
Poiseth his pinions
Ere over the waters
He moves like a vision
On motionless wings.

Beautiful, beautiful,
The sunlit gleam of her naked body,
Ivorywhite mid the cyclamen-blossoms,
A wave o' the sea mid the blooms of the Daphne
Blue as the innermost heart of the ocean

The arch of the sky where the wood runneth seaward,
Blue as the depths of the innermost heaven
The vast heaving breast of the slow-moving waters :
Green the thick grasses that run from the woodland,
Green as the heart of the foam-crested billows
Curving a moment ere washing far inland
Up the long reach of the sands gleaming golden.
The land-breath beareth
Afar the fragrance
Of thyme and basil
And clustered rosemary ;
And o'er the fennel,
And through the broom,
It floateth softly,
As the wind of noon
That cometh and goeth
Though none hearkens
Its downy wings.
And keen, the seawind
Bears up the odours
Of blossoming pinks
And salt rock-grasses,
Of rustling seaweed
And mosses of pools
Where the rosy blooms
Of the sea-flowers open
Mid stranded waves.
As a water-lily
Touched by the breath
Of sunrise-glory,
Moveth and swayeth

With tremulous joy,
So o'er the sunlit
White gleaming body
Of the beautiful bather
Passeth a quiver.
Rosy-white, as a cloud at the dawning,
Poised like a swallow that meeteth the wind,
For a moment she standeth
Where the seawind softly
Moveth over
The thick pink sward of the cyclamen-blossoms.
Moveth and rustleth
With faint susurrus
The pale pink blooms
Of the fragrant Daphne.

AT VEII

(" *Crown of Etruria* ")

Loud bloweth the Tramontana
O'er the uplands of Veii:
Shrill through the grasses
It whistles blithely,
Tossing the thistle-foam
Far o'er the pastures
Where the goat-skinn'd shepherd
Tendeth his sheep,
And the high hawk, swooping,
Drifteth his shadow
From slope to slope.

Here, when Rome lay
Crouch'd in her hollows
Where the Tiber lapped
The Hill of Saturn,
Veii the beautiful gleamed in the sunlight.
Here, in the springs
That bloomed as sweetly
Two thousand years since,

As now when the blackbird
Calleth loudly
Where the Cremera surgeth
Through her hollow glen,
And rainbows are woven
Where the torrents vanish
Over mossed ledges,
White sheets of water
With emerald hearts:
Here, the Etrurian
Banner waved proudly,
Lordly and glorious,
Sovereign ever
From sea to sea.
Here the proud hosts
Laughed when the battle-cry
Rang through the highways,
And when from the towers
Of Veii the mighty
The herald-clarions
Sent a wild blast
On the wind of the morning,
A tumult of summons
To the flashing swords,
And the merciless rain
Of spears gleaming white
As hail on the hill-sides.
Here the fair city was decked as a maiden
Led forth as a bride,
With sunlit towers
And banners yellow

With virgin gold,
And shrines of the holy ones
Aflame in the sun,
As the waters of ocean
When the blossom of morning
Swiftly unfolds in a myriad wavelets
Leaping and laughing in shining splendour.

Here now the dust bloweth
Where the Gods stood proudly,
Staring undaunted
Through the shadows of Tiber:
Here now the grasses
Wave, where the banners
Of ancient Etruria
Tossed i' the sun:
And where the clarions
Of the heralds rang,
The jay screameth
From her swaying bough.
Slowly the shepherd,
Like the moving shadow
Cast by the flock that followeth after,
Wandereth, heedless,
O'er the vast spaces:
Nor dreameth ever
Of what lies buried
Beneath the waste,
Though oft he wonders
When his foot striketh

A rusty spear-head;
Or when, from the mould,
A stone hand cometh,
As though the dead
Were stirring again
Where now the windblown foam of the thistles
Whitens the pastures of what was Veii.

THE WILD MARE

LIKE a breath that comes and goes
O'er the waveless waste
Of sleeping Ocean,
So sweeps across the plain
The herd of wild horses.
Like banners in the wind
Their flying tails,
Their streaming manes:
And like spume of the sea
Fang'd by breakers,
The white froth tossed from their bloodred nostrils.
Out from the midst of them
Dasheth a white mare,
White as a swan in the pride of her beauty:
And, like the whirlwind,
Following after,
A snorting stallion,
Swart as an Indian
Diver of coral!
Wild the gyrations,
The rush and the whirl;
Loud the hot panting
Of the snow-white mare,
As swift upon her

The stallion gaineth:
Fierce the proud snorting
Of him, victorious:
And loud,swelling loud on the wind from the mountains,
The hoarse savage tumult of neighing and stamping
Where, wheeling, the herd of wild horses awaiteth—
Ears thrown back, tails thrashing their flanks or swept
                                        [under—
The challenging scream of the conqueror-stallion.

AUGUST AFTERNOON IN ROME

(From the Trastevere)

[TO THÉODORE ROUSSEL]

DULL yellow shot with molten gold
The Tiber flows.
Beneath the walls the flood moves azurely,
With purplish shadows where the bridge
Spans triple-arch'd the stream:
Brown on the hither bank an idle barge,
With tawny sails still damp with spray
Blown from Ligurian seas:
And far, in the middle-flood, adrift, unoar'd,
A narrow boat, swift-moving, black,
Follows the flowing wave like a living thing.

Full-flooded by the sun the houses lie
Across the stream.
Pale pink their walls, or touched to paler blue,
But wanly yellow most, or soft as cream
Brown-curdled in the heat.
Oft, too, the tall façades asleep in the glow,
Are dusk'd by violet shadows, delicate
As the pale sheen of hyacinth-meadows where

The hills are glad with April wandering by.
Enmassed they stand, aglow, asleep:
The green blinds closed, like folded leaves,
Like ivy-leaves close-cluster'd to the pale white bark
Of the tall Austral trees belov'd of those
Who dwell where the Three Fountains rise from
[deathly soil.
Hot in the yellow glare of the sun they stand,
The myriad houses, with their infinite hues.

The green blinds here loom dark:
Here emerald-bright as the young grass that springs
Beneath the blackthorn-blossoms snowing down.
Brown-black the flat bare roofs,
Save where, like floating flower-clouds, gardens glow
High-perch'd mid perilous ravines of wall,
With scarlet, orange, white, and fleeting gold.
In the deserted streets no passer-by
Throws a distorted phantom o'er the way,
Though in the deep-blue shadow-side there drifts
A trickling stream of life.
Dim drowsy silence holds the day, for all
The water-seller sounding hollowly
His *Fresca, acqua fresca, fred' e fresc'!*
Or melon-merchant shrilling loud and thin
His long fantastic cry.

Here, silence too:
Only the long slow wash
Of the dull wave of Tiber's murmurous flood.
At times a far-off bell

Clangs,
And stillness comes again, as mists draw in.
Only the muffled voice
Of the wan, yellow, listless-moving stream—
And, hark, from yonder osteria, dim in shade,
The sudden, harsh, and dissonant jarring chords
Of a loose-strung guitar,
Twang'd idly for a few brief moments, ere
The half-sung song grows drowsier, and still.

THE OLIVES OF TIVOLI

GREY as the swirl
Of spindrift flying
O'er windblown ice,
Gleam the myriad leaves of the olives,
When, surging from under,
The wind leapeth
And laughs amongst them.
Like the sea when the tides
Are lifting and rippling
The restless wavelets
Wandering shoreward,
When over them breaketh
In a glittering shining
The flood of moonlight,
So are the wind-twisted olives of Tivoli.
Green as the grasses
When Scirocco bloweth
Palely upon them,
The lower leaves:
But soft and white
As the down of an owlet,
Or wan grey feathery plumes of the snow-flakes,
The myriad upper
Shimmering wings

That wave like surf o'er the sea of the olives,
When, surging from under,
Where the plain darkles
In purpling mist,
The wind laughs
As he leapeth among them.

SCIROCCO

(June)

SOFTLY as feathers
That fall through the twilight
When wild swans are winging
Back to the northward:
Softly as waters,
Unruffled, and tideless,
Laving the mosses
Of inland seas:
Soft through the forest,
And down through the valley,
Light as a breath o'er the pools of the marish,
Still as a moonbeam over the pastures,
Goeth Scirocco.

Warm his breath:
The night-flowers know it,
Love it, and open
Their blooms for its sweetness:
Warm the tender low wind of his pinions
Scarce brushing together the spires of the grasses:
Ah, how they whisper, the little green leaflets
Black in the dusk or grey in the moonlight:

Ah, how they whisper and shiver, the tremulous
Leaves of the poplar, and shimmer and rustle
When soft as a vapour that steals from the marshes
The wings of Scirocco fan silently through them.

Ofttimes he lingers
By ruined nests
Deep in the hedgerows,
And bloweth a feather
In little eddies,
A yellow feather
That once had fluttered
On a breast alive with
A rapture of song:
But slowly ceaseth,
And passeth sadly.
Ofttimes he riseth
Up through the branches
Where the fireflies wander,
Up through the branches
Of oak and chestnut,
And stirs so gently
With sway of his wings
That the leaves, dreaming,
Think that a moonbeam
Only, or moonshine,
Moves through the heart of them.
Upward he soareth
Oft, silently floating
Through the purple ether,
Still as the fern-owl over the covert,

Or as allocco haunting the woodland,
Up to the soft curded foam of the cloudlets,
The white dappled cloudlets the south-wind bringeth.
There, dreaming, he moveth
Or sails through the moonlight,
Till chill in the high upper air and the silence,
Slowly he sinketh
Earthward again,
Silently floateth
Down o'er the woodlands:
Foldeth his wings and slow through the branches
Drifts, scarcely breathing,
Till tired, mid the flowers or the hedgerows he creepeth,
Whispers alow mid the spires of the grasses,
Or swooning at last to motionless slumber
Floats like a shadow adrift on the pastures.

THE WIND AT FIDENAE

(To D. H. In Remembrance)

FRESH from the Sabines,
The Beautiful Hills,
The wind bloweth.
Down o'er the slopes,
Where the olives whiten
As though the feet
Of the wind were snow-clad:
Out o'er the plain
Where a paradise
Of wild blooms waveth,
And where, in the sunswept
Leagues of azure,
A thousand larks are
As a thousand founts
Mid the perfect joy of
The depths of heaven.
Swift·o'er the heights,
And over the valleys
Where the grey oxen sleepily stand,
Down, like a wild hawk swooping earthward,
Over the winding reaches of Tiber,
Bloweth the wind!

How the wind bloweth,
Here on the steeps of
Ancient Fidenae,
Where no voice soundeth
Now, save the shepherd
Calling his sheep;
And where none wander
But only the cloud-shadows,
Vague ghosts of the past.
Sweet and fresh from the Sabines.
Now as of yore,
When Etruscan maidens
Laughed as their lovers
Mocked the damsels
Of alien Rome,
Sweet with the same young breath o' the world
Bloweth the wind.

SORGENDO LA LUNA

No sound,
Save the hush'd breath,
The slowly flowing,
The long and low withdrawing breath of Rome.
Not a leaf quivers, where the dark,
With eyes of rayless shadow and moonlit hair,
Dreams in the black
And hollow cavernous depth of the ilex-trees.
No sound,
Save the hush'd breath of Rome,
And sweet and fresh and clear
The bubbling, swaying, ever quavering jet
Of water fill'd with pale nocturnal gleams,
That, in the broad low fount,
Falleth,
Falleth and riseth,
Riseth and falleth, swayeth and surgeth, ever
A spring of life and joy where ceaselessly
The shadow of two sovran powers make
A terror without fear, a night that hath no dark,
Time, with his sunlit wings,
Death, with his pinions vast and duskily dim:
Time, breathing vanishing life:
Death, breathing low
From twilights of Oblivion whence Time rose

A wild and wandering star forlornly whirled,
Seen for a moment, ere for ever lost.
Up from the marble fount
The water leaps,
Sways in the moonshine, springeth, springeth,
Falleth and riseth,
Like sweet faint lapping music,
Soft gurgling notes of woodland brooks that wander
Low laughing where the hollowed stones are green
With slippery moss that hath a trickling sound:
Leapeth and springeth,
Singing forever
A wayward song.
While the vast wings of Time and Death drift slowly,
While, faint and far, the tides of life
Sigh in a long scarce audible breath from Rome,
Or faintlier still withdraw down shores of dusk;
For ever singing
It leapeth and falleth:
Falleth and leapeth,
Falleth,
And falleth.

IN JULY

(South of Rome)

PALE-ROSE the dust lying thick upon the road:
Grey-green the thirsty grasses by the way.
The long flat silvery sheen of the vast champaign
Shimmers beneath the blazing tide of noon.
The bloodred poppies flame
Like furnace-breaths:
Like wan vague dreams the misty lavender
Drifts greyly through the quivering maze, or seems
Thus through the visionary glow to drift.
On the far slope, beyond the ruin'd arch,
A grey-white cloudlet rests,
The cluster'd sheep alow: close, moveless all,
And silent, save when faintly from their midst
A slumberous tinkle comes,
Cometh, and goeth.
Low-stretch'd in the blue shade,
Beneath the ruin,
The shepherd sleeps.
Nought stirs.
The wind moves not, nor with the faintest breath
Toucheth the half-fallen blooms of the asphodels.
Here only, where the pale pink ash
Of the long road doth slowly flush to rose,
A bronze-wing'd beetle moveth low,
And sends one tiny puff of smoke-like dust
Faint through the golden glimmer of the heat.

THE NAKED RIDER

THROUGH the dark gorge
With its cliffs of basalt,
The rider comes.
The sunlight floodeth
The breast of the hill,
And all the mouth
Of the sullen pass
Is light with the foam of
A thousand blooms
Of the white narcissi,
With a waving sea
Of asphodels.

On a white horse,
A cream-white stallion
With bloodred nostrils
And wild dark eyes,
The naked rider
Laughs as he cometh,
And hails the sunlight breaking upon him.
Full breaks the flood
Of the yellow light
On the naked youth,

Glowing, as ivory
In the amber of moonrise
In the violet eves
Of August-tides.
Dark as the heart of a hill-lake his tresses,
Scarlet the crown of the poppies inwoven
I' the thick wavy hair that crowneth his whiteness,
Strong the white arms,
The broad heaving breast,
The tent thighs guiding
The mighty stallion.

Out from the gloom
Of the mountain valley,
Where cliffs of basalt
Make noontide twilight,
And where the grey bat
Swingeth his heavy wings,
And echo reverberates
The screams of the falcons:
Where nought else soundeth
Save the surge or the moaning
Of mountain-winds,
Or the long crash and rattle
Of falling stones
Spurned by the hill fox
Seeking his hollow lair:
Out from the gorge
Into the sunlight,
To the glowing world,
To the flowers and the birds

And the west wind laden
With the breaths of rosemary, basil, and thyme —
Comes the white rider,
The naked youth
Glowing like ivory
In the yellow sunshine.
Beautiful, beautiful, this youth of the mountain,
Laughing low as he rideth
Forth to the sunlight,
The scarlet poppies agleam in his tresses
Dark as the thick-cluster'd grapes of the ivy;
While over the foam
Of the sea of narcissi,
And high through the surf
Of the asphodels,
Trampleth, and snorteth
From his bloodred nostrils,
The cream-white stallion.

THE FALLEN GODDESS

(On a Statue of Venus, found near Anzio (Antium) *on the
Latin Coast, and now in a Church as the Madonna
of the Seven Sorrows)*

Not here, O Goddess,
In these chill glooms
With silence about thee—
Save when at matins or dusk o' the evensong
The priests mutter
Or chant the Mass,
And the few tired peasants
Pray with bent heads,
Lost in the stillness,
Lost in the gloom —
Not here, O Goddess,
Thy resting-place,
Who, ages ago,
When the world was young,
Stood where the myrtles and roses were blooming,
Stood where the dayshine was rising and flooding
Up from the purple-blue flower of the ocean,
Flooding and rising till all of the inland
Glowed in the splendour, and valley and mountain
Laughed with the joy of the world's young laughter.

Ah, when about thee,
The roses were twined,
When thy feet were covered
With roses and lilies,
When low before thee,
Fresh pluckt by thy fountain,
Lay sweet-smelling violets —
And, kneeling before thee,
The lovers prayed,
He wan as ivory
Found where the sources
Of Nilus wander
In swart Ethiopia,
She as the nenuphar
Waked by the moonlight
Flooding the river, as
Duskily moving
In coils gigantic
It flows through the desert,
Where the Sphinx broodeth
And where, at dawn,
The voice of Memnon
Solemnly calls —
Ah, when beside thee,
The lovers prayed,
And thy heart was stirred
With the wind of their love,
With passion and longing
And sweet desire —
Ah, in that moment,
Did some dark shadow

From Time unborn
Dusk thy glad vision?
Didst thou, upon them,
Kneeling before thee,
Frown, and heed not
The prayer they made:
In thy heart the ache
And a deathless sorrow
That made their passion
A bitter folly?
What unto thee, then,
O Venus, Goddess,
The roses and lilies
Entwined about thee,
The fragrant violets
Freshly gathered
With the spray o' thy fountain
Dew-sprent o'er them;
What then to thee
Thy myrtle-grove,
Thy doves and sparrows
Fluttering about thee,
Fluttering, flying
Through the azure air —
What, O Goddess,
Thy worshippers pale,
He with the passion
Aflame in his eyes,
She with the longing
Astir in her bosom,
Whose two white flowers

Are pressed against thee
Where the violets cover
And cloud thy feet?
Foresawest thou ever,
At morn or dusk,
With lovers praying
And garlanding thee
With the flowers thou lovest,
Or when in the silent
Depths o' the night
Thy vigils knew not
A stir, a whisper,
But all was darkness
And brooding peace,
Forsawest thou ever
Thy doom to be?
The veils of darkness
That yet would cover
The earth thou lovest,
The passing of all
The joyous gods,
And slowly, slowly
Across the world
The chilling shadow
Fall of the Cross?

Ah, better that after
Thy doom had fallen
And thenceforth lovers
Sought thee no more,
And only the wild doves

Hovered about thee,
Only the sparrows
Out of the wildwood
Fluttered about thine uncrown'd forehead,
Only the wild-rose clambered around thee,
Only the hyacinths out of the woodland
Stole through the grasses
And decked thee and girt thee —
Better that after
The fierce barbarians
Thrust thee prostrate
With laughter and mocking,
And left thee, there,
In the Groves of Venus,
A thing dishonoured,
A Fallen Goddess, —
Better that then
The weeds had gathered
And swift o'ergrown thee,
And leaves of autumn,
And dust o' the wind,
And earth and mosses,
Had swallowed thee up,
Had hidden thee ever,
There in thy sorrow,
There in thy dream,
With none to know of thee,
None to mourn,
Save only the wild-dove brooding alone,
Only the song-birds lost in the thicket,
Only the hyacinths, lilies, and roses,
Only the grasses that wave round thy fountain,

Only the violets, purple, sweet-smelling,
Deep in the heart of them, lost in their twilight.

Harsh fate for thee,
Goddess, not thus to have lain
In the mould and the darkness
Till at last, in the far-off,
The slow revolution
Of ages or eons
Should bring thee, awaking,
The sound of rejoicing !
When all thy white kindred
Should gather about thee,
With songs and laughter,
And greet thee, and bless thee,
And woo thee with longing and rapture and kisses,
While joyous behind them,
From mountain and valley
And up from the shores of
The vast flower of Ocean,
White-robed lovers should hasten and follow,
Hands claspt in hands,
With baskets of roses
And lilies for thee,
And doves soft and snowwhite
As these, thy white breasts,
And prayers, and incense
Of violets fragrant,
Fresh-gathered violets smelling of thee:
Then, then, would'st thou stir
In the dark mould about thee,

And sweet in the woodland
The wild-doves would murmur,
And swift in the thicket the song-birds would gather,
And all from about thee the darkness would lessen.
Up through the grasses, and where the wild hyacinths
Cluster enmassed in a hollow of blueness,
And where the wild-roses are raining their petals
Down through the fragrant green boughs of their tangle
Up through the midst of them, white as a seabird
Rising from out of the joy of the billows,
Swift would arise, like a flower too, thine arm:
Then from the tangle of roses and grasses —
O but the joy of it ! white gleaming shoulders,
Head with the halo of empire about it,
Eyes deep with the dream of the secrets of life,
And firm breasts white as the milk held within
                                        [them—
O body of beauty, O Venus, O Goddess
Thus, thus would thy birth be, thy glad resurrection!

Ah better that after
Thy doom had fallen
Thou hadst not waken'd,
O Goddess, more!
Better that never
The Roman warriors
Staring upon thee
Beheld thy beauty
And laughed to see it,
And took thee and haled thee
Far from thy grove,

And girt thee with rushes and flags from the sea-shore,
And laid thee a captive deep down in a war-boat,
And heedless of wrath or of vengeance from heaven
Carried thee far through the waters Ionian,
Up through the wide lonely waste of the Tyrrhene,
Till dim through the haze, like a cloud at the dawning,
The low shores of Latium
Blue rose before thee.

Was it for this,
O Venus, Goddess,
That thou hast passioned?
O bitter lust
Of a joyless faith,
That mocketh beauty
And laudeth the grave:
What thing is this,
What bitter mocking,
That thou hast taken
The sacred Goddess
And raised her darkling
Here in thy temple,
Midst tawdry idols
And childish things—
Hast placed upon her
Immaculate brows
This tinsel crown;
And hung about her
These pitiful robes
That a slave would have scorned
In the olden days

When men loved beauty
For beauty's sake:
Hast decked her bosom
(O Heart of Love!)
With a thing shaped heart-wise
And seven times pierced
With brazen arrows.
Hast stolen thy name, even, Goddess, Venus,
And called thee Mother
Of a God thou know'st not,
Called thee Madonna, the Mother of Sorrows,
Called thee the Virgin of Sorrows Seven—
Was it for this—
Ah, better a thousand times
They had wrought thy havoc,
There, in the heart of
Thy sacred grove:
Better—O bitterness
Of things that are,
Goddess, and Queen!

DE PROFUNDIS

WHENCE hast thou gone,
O vision belovëd?
There is silence now
In thy groves, and never
A voice proclaimeth
Thy glory come,
Thy joy rearisen!

O passion of beauty,
Forsake not thus
Those who have worshipped thee,
Body and soul!
Come to us, come to us,
Inviolate, Beautiful,
Thou whose breath
Is as Spring o'er the world,
Whose smile is the flowering
Of the wide green Earth!
Deep in the heart of thee,
Like a moonbeam moving
Through the heart of a hill-lake,
Moveth Compassion:
O Belovëd,
Be with us ever,
Thou, the Beautiful,
Passion of Beauty,
Alma Victrix!

ULTIMO SOSPIRO

O dolce primavera pien' di olezzo e amor!
Che fai tu..... che fai fra tanti fior?

Colgo le rose amabili dei più soavi odori;
Colgo le rose affabili e i lunghi gelsomini,
Nei olenti miei giardini io vi tengo al cor.
                              ROMAN FOLKSONG.

Joy of the world,
O flower-crown'd Spring,
With thine odorous breath and thy heart of love,
Breathe through this verse thy sweet message of longing.
Lo, in the groves of Dream, whose lovers
Die gladly in worship, but fail not ever,
Oft have I strayed,
Oft have I lingered
When high through the noon the lost lark has been
                                        [singing,
Or when in the moonlight
Soft through the silence has whispered the ocean,
Or when, in the dark
Of the ilex-woods,
Where the fireflies wavered
Frail wandering stars,
Not a sound has been heard
But Scirocco rustling
The midmost leaves
Of the trees where he sleepeth.

Roses of love,
White lilies of dream,
Frail blooms that have blossom'd
Into life with thy breathing:
Blow them, O wind,
West wind of the Spring,
Lift them and take them where gardens await them,
Lift them and take them to those who hearken,
Facing the dawn, for the sounds of the morning,
With wide eyes glad with the beautiful vision,
O whispers of joy,
O breaths of passion,
O sighs of longing.

Epilogue

IL BOSCO SACRO

(TO————————————————)

Ah, the sweet silence:
Not a breath stirreth:
Scarce a leaf moveth.

The Dusk, as a dream,
Steals slowly, slowly,
With shadowy feet
Under the branches
Here, in the woodland,
Hushfully seeking
The Night, her lover.

Sweet are the odours
Breath'd through the twilight,
Lovely spirits
Of lovely things.
One by one
Forth-shimmer white stars
Beyond the skiey
Boughs of the chestnuts,
Pale phosphorescence

Gleaming and glancing
As in the wake
Of a windspent vessel
That, moonlike, drifts
With motionless motion.

Peace : utter peace.
Not a sound riseth
From where in the hollow
The town lies dreaming :
Not a cry from the pastures
That far below
Are drowsed in the shadows.
Only afar,
On the dim Campagna,
Peace, utter peace :
On the pastures, peace ;
Low in the hollows,
Deep in the woodlands,
High on the hill-slopes,
Rest, utter rest,
Utter peace.

Suddenly . . . . . . thrilling
Long-drawn vibrations !
Passionate preludes
Of passionate song !
O the wild music
Tost through the silence,
As a swaying fountain
Is swept by the wind's wings
Far through the sunshine,

A mist of flashing
And falling spray.
How the hush of the stillness
Deepeneth slowly . . . . . .
Till never, never
Can pain and rapture
So wild a music,
So sweet a song,
List in the moonlight—
Listen again
O never, never !

O heart, still thy beating :
O bird, thy song !
Too deep the rapture
Of this new sorrow.
White falls the moonshine
Here, where we gather'd
The snow-pure blossoms,
The Flowers of Dream :
Here, when the sunlight
On that glad day
Flooded the mosses
With golden wine,
And deep in the forest
Joy passed us, laughing,
Laughing low,
While ever behind her
Rose lovely, delicate,
Beautiful, beautiful,
The fadeless blossoms,
The Flowers of Dream.

Be still, O beating,
O yearning heart!
Here there is silence ......
Silence ...... Silence ......
O beating heart!

Here, in the sunshine,
Together we gather'd
The perfect blooms:
And now in the gloaming,
Here, where the moonlight,
Lies like white foam on
The dark tides of night,
Here is one only,
Longing forever,
Longing, longing
With passion and pain.

Come, O Belovëd!
O heart, be still!
Nay, through the silence
Cometh no answer,
But only, only
The sweet subsiding
Of this wild strain
Now lost in the thickets
Down in the hollows.

Hark ...... rapture outwelling!
O song of joy!
Glad voice of my passion

Singing there
Out of the heart of
The fragrant darkness!
O flowers at my feet,
White beautiful flowers,
That whisper, whisper
My soul's desire!
O never, never
Lost though afar,
My Joy, my Dream!

Too deep the rapture
Of this sweet sorrow,
Of this glad pain:
O heart, still thy beating,
O bird, thy song!